Through the Grinder, Darkly

The Best of the 2K Terrors Competition 2023

www.tldrpress.org

Through the Grinder, Darkly: The Best of the 2K Terrors Competition

First published in 2024

Table of Contents

Necromancy, and Other Fun Games You Can Play at Home

Bryan Arneson

Vlogger | A Ritual

Aiden's eye stings.

It's somewhere between the tangy, chemical burn of shampoo and the blinking, biting irritation of sweat. He tries to rub his sleeve across the damp skin, but his trembling muscles are too busy collapsing into the fetal position, so instead, his hand passes under his running nose, mixing snot with the hot fluid soaking into his distressed *Ramones* t-shirt.

It's blood.

Of course, he already *knew* it was blood, but as Aiden blinks and follows the crimson trail from his head to his sleeve to the carpet running under his bedroom door and into the hall of his parents' house, that's when it really hits him, the idea sinking in like the slow sucking of sand in the shallows of a tidal beach.

"Mom and dad are gonna kill me…" Aiden moans the words like a kid trying to stay home from school and feels the echo of them in his stomach, wrestling his gut like a belch that refuses to come up.

Taking a deep, shivering breath, Aiden winces and shifts onto his hip and elbow. His left hand holds his cell phone in a death grip, fingers zombie-white as he swipes the screen. The image is distorted under a red smear, and Aiden wipes the now cracked glass with the hem of his t-shirt, grimacing as he only succeeds in turning a straight smudge into a swirly one.

Outside his room a scraping bumping roll rumbles past, like someone moving out the family furniture without watching for corners and walls. Aiden tries not to think about it. One thing at a time. He rubs his phone screen face-down on the carpet of his bedroom floor, moving the stain from the cracked glass to the potato-chip-dusted fibers.

Swipe. Tap. Focus. Record.

"Things…" Aiden's voice is hoarse and he leans his chin back, working his jaw and swallowing hard to loosen it back up. "Update Post: Things have gotten… out of hand."

Aiden flinches as a rapid, skittering thud, like some mastiff-sized centipede, careens through the hallway outside, sending the bathrobe on the back of his door gently swaying from the tremors. Distantly, he hears the abrupt scream of a cat yowling and a crunch not unlike biting into firm celery. Aiden winces, choking as he whispers, "Sorry, Muffin."

Shifting to his knees, Aiden keeps his phone camera angled to his face. He grabs his desk for support but lets out a gasp of pain and jerks his palm back. Turning his fingers over, he sees a large shard of glass embedded between his 'love line' and 'life line', both now weeping blood around the thick, sharp chip.

He grits his teeth and removes the smaller fragments of mirror from his twitching hand. "I'm not sure what I did wrong. Maybe nothing? I mean, *something* is here, so I must have done it right. At least mostly right… Yay me."

Aiden drops the littler shards to his desktop with thin *ticks*, droplets of blood following like garnish on a fancy restaurant plate. He tilts the cell phone down to capture the image, flinching and feeling the stab of the larger splinter still embedded in the skin of his palm as he fights to keep the phone steady. "I dropped the mirror… so I'm not sure how I get it back where it came from. Can I use a different mirror?"

Trying to keep his voice steady, Aiden is infuriatingly aware of his phone's dead internet connection. The camera seems to work, but just the fact that it was going to be a vlog post instead of live-streamed would cast doubt that it was anything but camera tricks and CGI. He supposes that was one reason to survive.

Post or perish.

"The bathroom." Aiden mimes a stiff snap with his injured fingers. "The bathroom mirror should be big enough. I think...? If it's a bunch of little mirrors in the same frame, does that count as one mirror?"

Outside his door, the kitchen pans rattle and clatter, accompanied by more rambunctious skittering. It's on the other side of the house now, he realizes, and Aiden doesn't have time to think. Closing his phone, he dashes to his door.

He'd lost the *thing* by hiding in his bedroom, so he knew it could be evaded.

On hands and knees, Aiden pushes the door open, crawling out. His stinging palm makes him shake and wince with every crawling step, but he keeps his whimpers silent as he moves foot by agonizing foot up the hallway to the bathroom.

The house is swallowed in a cavernous darkness, an oppressive, unrelenting black that permits no star or moon to intercede on behalf of breathing creatures. The only light is the dim glow of the ritual candles set around his mother's charcuterie board on the kitchen table, and the dull reflection those wicks give the vacation photos framed along the main hall.

Aiden had stumbled to the bathroom hundreds of times, still half-asleep and not bothering to find a switch. He knew it by feel even if he couldn't see the doorframe in the gloom ahead of him.

But as his eyes adjust, Aiden sees that the darkness surrounding him is not truly still. It's pulsing, breathing even, wheezing like an old man's death rattle. Now it sounds like the far off giggling of small children. Aiden shivers, crawling faster, but the blood pounding in his ears can't seem to drown out those sounds.

"Where is it?" Aiden squeaks, his palm reaching for the bathroom door and only finding more wall. "I should have found it by now." Fumbling for his phone, Aiden turns on the flashlight app.

Two luminous, unseeing eyes stare at him accusingly from the darkness. The wet matted fur and crooked teeth of what used to be Muffin the cat flops and slides forward, useless paws dragging on the carpet as it emerges from the breathing shadow. The cat's jaw pistons like a Christmas nutcracker as Aiden feels his arms and legs go numb with a sudden cold.

"You have freed me... what is your wish?" hisses a thin, respiratory voice.

Aiden freezes, stammering, "Wait. Really?"

"No." The voice breaks off into a cacophony of tumbling, spiraling laughter that seems to come from all sides, filling the spectrum from heavy, old belly-laughs to high and wiry children's titters. The cat puppet shivers and spins erratically in front of him, and Aiden throws himself back as the shadows launch the maimed carcass into his chest with an almost playful *thop*.

Hurtling to the front door, Aiden wrestles the handle, leaving streaks of bloody handprints as he pounds the glass and screams for help. But he knows he's wasting time. The glass is as cold as winter frost and where streetlights and the headlamps of passing cars should have filled the dark between the stars, instead there is simply... nothing.

The coiling darkness skitters over the walls, blotting out the twinkling of reflected candlelight and swallowing the house's creaking with its own insectile movements. The wheezing, vapor-thin speaker teases, "Run, run, run, as fast as you can," in a dissonant chorus of voices that feel as stolen as the feline corpse it had manipulated in the hall. Rising up, the darkness forms a writhing current, flooding down the hall like drain water, intent on flushing Aiden away.

Throwing himself into the kitchen, Aiden screams, the wave splashing against the front door with a sound like a slowly spilled box of tacks.

"Stay back! Be thee bound! Uh, the power of Christ— shit!" Aiden falls against the kitchen table as a tendril of darkness sweeps toward him like a striking viper. He fumbles for the ritual circle, its light illuminating the shattered mirror, what was disturbingly only *mostly* his own blood, and his mother's charcuterie board, pulling away a candle.

He hurls the lit flame at the shadow, watching in horror as the lit wick immediately suffocates.

"Come ON!"

The darkness spreads over the kitchen walls, expanding like a time-lapse of black mold consuming the room around him.

Articulate thought collapsing in the face of desperate, panicked instinct, Aiden shoves the kitchen cupboards open, dragging rattling boxes of pasta and heavy cans of sauce to the floor as he claws through them.

"Oregano, parsley, cumin, *sage!*" Removing the lid from the spice shaker, he pours a fistful of ground sage into his blood-caked hand and squats behind the candles. With a loud, cheek-puffing exhalation, Aiden blows the dried herb across the flame, watching the dust cloud of miniature leaf fragments catch fire in small eruptions of orange as they fill the air with a fragrant scent.

The tablecloth swiftly catches fire and for a brief instant, the room is lit by a stronger light. Aiden's spine stiffens, and he lets out a tiny squeak.

The writhing darkness around him is filled with innumerable faces. Old and young, plump and drawn, all of them cast in the flare of the tablecloth's fire like bas reliefs in some ancient, moldering wall. The faces contort, horror and fear causing their features to stretch and collapse in a thousand shrieking cries.

A coil of darkness comes down on the table, shattering the circle of candles and dousing the tablecloth in an instant. Aiden screams as shards of glass from the broken mirror fly with the impact, covering his upraised arms and hands. One by one, the candles spilling over the ground roll into the encroaching shadow and are snuffed out.

With nothing else to do, and the darkness only a few feet from him, Aiden snatches a large can of iodized salt and pours a hurried circle, falling into it cross-legged as he huddles to the ground.

The last candle goes out.

Wheezing darkness.

Sharp shards of glass cover him, and Aiden feels the heartbeat pulse of his blood running from fresh cuts.

He's alive.

With trembling hands, Aiden winces and draws out his cell phone. Maybe half a meter of space inside his circle of salt… everything else is the darkness—blinking, staring, gasping as if the hundred faces in its shadowy folds cannot catch their breath.

Looking down, Aiden watches the granules of salt drifting with those breaths like sand being washed away on a beach. His heart drums and he blinks at the eroding salt line.

Swipe. Tap. Focus. Record.

"…Update—Last Update Post… probably." Aiden rotates the camera, watching the footage on his cellphone distort with digital corruption until he brings it back around to his face. "I'm trapped in a… disintegrating… circle of salt… If I had any advice for people thinking about trying the ritual themselves at home… Don't. I guess?" Aiden gives a weak laugh, shuddering as a tendril of darkness pokes a weak portion of his salt barrier. "Well, looks like my time's about up. Smash that Like button and—"

The circle breaks; a line of darkness floods in like the pressurized gout from a garden hose. Aiden screams and raises his wounded hands, dropping his cell phone.

…

The next video on the playlist starts. The cell phone is propped on Aiden's bedroom desk and pointing up as Aiden stares intently at his hand then back into the camera.

"Ok, tell the internet what you just told me."

A swirl of clicking darkness spirals in Aiden's left eye, and his jaw works with doll-like stiffness as he lets out a long, wheezing sigh. "Very well… yes, any number of glasses within the same frame count as *one* mirror."

"And my body is, like, the frame?" Lifting his palm, Aiden shakes his head at the reflective shard embedded in it, turning it to the camera.

"Yes, man-mirror," the voice in him hisses darkly. "If I am the genie, *you* are the lamp."

Form Of

Kat Veldt

Philosopher | A Deed to a House

The most recent electric bill is on the upper bound of normal. But this is a *new* house, which the executor said the way people usually say *old* house, so much so that it took Sashka a beat to realize what she'd actually heard. Old houses eat and stay hungry, is what the executor told her, but new houses are built with big bellies. No one has been here for two weeks, and Sashka's still going to have to pay an upper-bound electric bill. He found a way to leave her less than nothing.

It's not like she'll live here. This thing was built to be a background in a photograph on the inside flap of a dust jacket. These big tall shelves, floor to ceiling. They look like they should be for show, but Sashka pulls one random book off the shelf, and there are all his chicken scratches crammed in the margins, a dialogue five hundred years too late for anyone to answer. Another one, another pen color, notes and notes and notes.

Full bookshelves, empty fridge, stripped mattress. They do that as a courtesy, when they find somebody. He was there long enough to leave a stain, so they took the sheets and the mattress cover and shoved them in a biohazard bag. Disinfected the room, opened the windows to air out the smell. They let Sashka see a photo of the body in situ, when she asked. The perfect looming Form of Dead, qualified and conditioned into this imperfect mirror of a mirror that was sort of boring to look at, all things considered. An old man on his back. Her imagination would have come up with worse.

She sits down in the middle of the mattress for a while, crosses her legs. He was here for days. Would've been longer, if he hadn't missed a speaking engagement for the first time in sixty years.

They gave her a blueprint along with the deed, and she spreads it out on the floor of the bedroom. There's supposed to be a finished basement, they gave her a whole drawing of it, except she can't find any stairs on the map or in real life. Presumably they're behind the locked door down the hall from the bedroom, but the only key she has is the one to the front. When she asked about it, the office told her they'd look into the documentation to see if they missed any assets in the transfer. Maybe it really was just a clerical error, and the key is in somebody's drawer somewhere. Maybe there's a hollowed-out book on the sitting room shelves, and the key is hidden inside. Maybe he realized he was on his way out and swallowed it, and no one thought to cut him open and check around for clues. Sashka can't really ask the executors for help with the last option. They already stare at her when they think she's distracted.

She spends ten minutes googling locksmiths, then puts her phone down on top of her stack of butcher paper.

The house may be *new*, but a door is a door. Sashka gets her hammer and the long orange screwdriver from her car and unpins the hinges on the nearest locked door from bottom to top, levers them open with the claw, as gentle as she can be about it when the muscles in her arms are already starting to burn. This felt easier the last time she did it, but she'd been twenty-four, then. With the right motivation, she could have done anything.

He's not keeping his prescriptions behind this door - and even if he is, he never had the good stuff, anyway. He stood on the shore while Sashka drank from her mother's ocean of codeine and said, not I. Let my joints fall out of their sockets. Let my nerves turn against me. I'll feel every organ fail, one at a time. And then he wondered why Sashka never came around.

Well, she's here now, in a room full of equipment, some of which is active, probably drawing an upper-bound-normal amount of power.

"Jesus," she says to no one.

The computers are password-protected, but he's been using the same password since before computers existed. Oh-eight one-five eight-three. Sashka watched a recording of him explaining to an audience as an aside, creases around his eyes while he typed it in, the imperfect human version of the Form of Lecturer. He gave them a line about using Timaeus as a bedtime story. They chuckled like they thought he was joking.

She logs into the nearest laptop. There are documents open: a bunch of medical records, at a glance. The backlog of an EKG feed. Maybe he was sicker than anybody realized. He chose decomposing in his bed over giving anyone else the key to this door.

There's another door on the other side of the room. Sashka unhinges it. There are stairs behind it, so she takes them down.

Whoever was here last left all the lights on. He put a second kitchen down here for some reason, refrigerator plugged in and humming, bulbs hanging in a line above the granite island. It's not messy, but it's not tidy, either. Dishes stacked in the sink. A loaf of bread twist-tied on the counter. Sashka walks through and into the main hallway.

The blueprint showed three rooms, but the hall has two doors on the right, two on the left, and one at the end. Sashka brought her hammer and screwdriver, just in case, but door number one on the right is unlocked, and it's a bathroom. Pastel but warm, the way Sashka's mother would have done it. An orange shower curtain with white and yellow circles all over. A handsoap pump shaped like a frog. She shuts the door again.

Door number one on the left is locked. Sashka's knees aren't going to put up with much more, but she makes it into an office. The kind of old, austere room that felt too big for its walls when she was younger. This might actually be the same desk she used to peek around. The Form of His Desk, so faithfully materialized that when she puts her palm on the surface, it's exactly as cool as she expects it to be.

There are documents and texts, post-it notes held in place with scotch tape, arranged in organized chaos, and in the center, not a document - a diary. Sashka's diary, the one she had when she was nine. The cover is orange and yellow. She'd picked it out herself, and he'd bought it for her, and she'd addressed the first couple of entries to him. It's open to the middle, careful block letters, *Dear*—maybe she'd held on longer than she remembers before she switched to Diary. *Today I did my coloring book. I watched TV. I thought you were home this week.*

Second door on the right is a linen closet. Towels, washcloths, a folded white robe. Shampoo with coconut and jojoba oil. Sanitary gauze and disposable cannulae. Sashka shuts the door. She goes back to the study and shuts the diary on the desk, while she's thinking about it.

She opens the second door on the left, and the girl behind it says, "Hi."

"Ah," Sashka says. "Hi."

The girl is sitting cross-legged in the middle of her orange bedspread. Uneven little braids over and around the crown of her head, yellow beads at the ends. They're about a week past when they should have been taken down. She says, "Are you lost?"

"No," Sashka says. "I don't think so. Is this your house?"

"I guess."

"What's your name?" Sashka asks her.

"Sashka."

"Okay," Saskha says. "Nice to meet you, Sashka."

"Is he coming down?" the girl asks her. "We're supposed to read. I think he forgot."

"I haven't seen him," Sashka says. "I'll remind him, if I do."

"Are you doing my medicine?" The girl holds out her arm, a tidy PICC line in the crook of her elbow.

"No," Sashka says, "that's okay. You can go to sleep, if you want."

She steps back into the hallway and closes the door. The girl doesn't protest at all.

There's a little examination room at the end of the hall. Girl-sized table under the ceiling lights, girl-sized stethoscopes and thermometers on the wall. A file of folders with filled-out forms, chicken scratch on the lines and in the margins. Growth charts and metabolic panels. Notes and notes and notes.

A locked safe on the counter next to the sink. Sashka birthdays it open. Four rows of divots, two still full of doses, dated and timed in his most careful print. There are three overdue. She shuts the safe again.

Sashka opens the second door on the left again and says, "Are you hungry, sweetheart?"

The girl shrugs. "I have sandwich stuff."

"We can do better than sandwich stuff," Sashka says. "Do you like bacon?"

That gets a smile, two big buck teeth. "I love bacon."

"I'll make you some bacon."

"Maybe later," the girl says. "I'm kind of - I don't know. I haven't felt so good."

"I bet you haven't."

"Can you read to me?"

"Yeah," Sashka says. "Sure."

She sits in an armchair next to the bed, right under an EKG monitor. There are books stacked on the nightstand. Not the same order Sashka got them in, back when there was still time for bedtime stories, but she recognizes the editions.

"D'you remember what you're reading together?" Sashka picks up the book on the top, asks, "Was it this one?"

The girl gets up on her knees, looks over Sashka's shoulder. "I think so," she says. "What's it called?"

"*Parmenides*. Do you like it so far?"

"I don't know," the girl says. "They're all fighting with each other."

"It's a dialogue," Sashka says. "They're not really mad. They're just thinking together."

"What're they thinking about?"

Sashka leans back in the chair. The girl's leads are long enough for her to climb off the bed and into Sashka's lap, wobbly foal legs tucked underneath her, head resting on Sashka's shoulder. Sashka's arm would fall asleep if they stayed like this, but kids are wiggly, she'll get her circulation back before she has a chance to miss it.

"I haven't read this one in a long time," Sashka says, "but I think they're trying to decide how things can be different but also the same. Like, how people can be different, but they can still all be people. Is each person different, or are they all versions of a perfect Person that we can never see?"

"Which one is it?"

Sashka tilts her head down until she can see the girl's face. "You wanna know the end before the middle?"

The girl reaches up and pokes Sashka's double chin.

"They don't know," Sashka says. "That's the end of it. They never make up their minds."

"Well, that's stupid."

"It seems kind of lazy, right? Making you read this whole big thing, and then he doesn't even tell you what he means. But actually," Sashka says, "he wants you to decide for yourself."

"What's your name?" the girl asks.

"Sashka," Sashka says.

"Oh." The girl smiles at her, sleepy. "Nice to meet you, Sashka. Do you know my dad?"

"I do," Sashka says.

"He's home this week. I finished my coloring book."

"You can show it to me later, if you want to."

There's a tremor in the girl's hands. Withdrawal, probably. They're going to want to get her under observation. She says, "I want to show my dad."

"I'll make sure he sees it," Sashka says. She rests her chin on the rows of shaky, inexpert braids. "I know he'll be really proud."

The Vast Enormity of the Sea

MM Schreier

Offshore Rig Worker | Adoption

Cold, quiet, dark. That's what I told landlubbers when they asked what diving was like. What I didn't say was how peaceful it was, especially the deeper I went. Just me and my thoughts and a passing eel or two.

I checked my depth gauge. Forty meters. Glancing up, I located my spotter. He hovered near the oil rig's massive metal leg about three meters above me—making an inky, finned silhouette in the darkness, an odd merman illuminated by the fading spotlight of his headlamp. I circled my forefinger and thumb, holding up my other three fingers in an *a-okay* gesture. He flipped me the bird. Not technically on the list of the Diver's Association's official hand signals.

Being the crew's underwater welder—the highest-paid diver on the rig—was one thing. The gall of holding that position as a woman was something else altogether. It hadn't made me a whole lot of drinking buddies.

Shrugging, I got back to work. I was an excellent welder, a better diver, and didn't need some asshole spotter to keep me safe.

My sheets are wet. Not night sweat damp, but cold and sopping. Despite the chill, I can't make myself move, only listen to the rhythmic plink-plonk of water dripping onto the floor. My brain struggles to understand what my body feels. How could someone dump an entire bucket of water on the bed and not wake me?

This is one prank too far. I've ignored the never-ending parade of half-rotten fish heads in my boots. I don't complain that somehow, I always get the gritty dregs of the coffee at breakfast. Screwing with my sleep, though, is the last straw. Diving tired makes you shark bait.

Still in my sodden pajamas, I stalk down the hall leaving a trail of wet footprints behind me. When I reach the Toolpusher's cabin I bang on the door. He's a mouse of a man, but surely, he'll do something. It's his rig to manage, his crew to wrangle.

He doesn't answer the door.

Coward.

I return to my bunk, but when I bend to strip the bedding, I realize it's dry. Is this part of the joke? It makes little sense. I flop down on the hard mattress, annoyed but too exhausted to do much else. Something pokes me in the shoulder. I fish around in the sheets and pull out a shell the size of a ping-pong ball. Not the wave-beaten, fractured bit of calcite that people oh and ah over on white sand beaches, but a fully spiraled nautilus.

My thoughts, fuzzy in that liminal space between waking and sleep, do not dwell on how such a thing ended up in my bed, but rather that I hope the critter who lived inside has moved out. I imagine the feel of tiny appendages on my cheek.

I'm sure it's all a dream.

Something brushed the back of my leg, softly but firm enough I could feel it through my dry suit. Amateur divers panicked, thrashing and churning in the water when the ocean reached out and touched them. Just like prey. Experienced divers stayed calm. And alive.

Without looking down, I flipped off the welding iron. Four hundred amps of direct current screamed through the electrode, and I had no interest in getting fried. Wet welding was far more dangerous than anything the ocean might tickle me with.

I blinked and double-checked the weld. Straight and even. I gave a thumbs up to my spotter and he reeled in the equipment. The jerk didn't bother to wait for me, but fins churning, swam straight up toward the first decompression stop. His light faded to a pinprick, then nothingness.

Another touch drew my attention. Slow and calm, I turned, bringing my headlamp around. A grayish-pink tentacle felt up my leg, gentle suckers exploring the seam in my dry suit. The octopus was massive with arms thicker than my thigh. My heart thudded in my ears. Another enormous tentacle wrapped around my waist.

I shuddered and reminded myself that octopuses were smart and curious, rarely aggressive to humans.

It pulled me closer until I was face to face with a dinner plate sized eye.

For the first time, I understood how sailors of old began rumors of the Kraken.

Everything tastes like brine, even the coffee. I grimace and set the mug down. Something wriggles in my bowl of stew. I look closer. A swarm of sea fleas backstroke in the broth and feast on the lumps of oversalted beef. I shove the bowl away, trying not to throw up.

I look around to see if anyone else notices the rancid food. The mess hall is nearly deserted, with only a handful of serious-faced diners sitting close together and whispering in low voices. No one looks at me. Fine. It's better than the sneers and scowls that usually come my way.

Everything's oddly quiet. I can feel the sway of the platform and the never-ceasing hum of the drilling equipment, but it's as if there's water in my ears. I tilt my head to the side, like an overgrown retriever, and hop, trying to shake the water out.

I've never had a dog. I figure I travel too much, and it wouldn't be fair for it to be always waiting for me to come home. It's a bit of a dream though, for retirement. People like me either retire early, bodies too beat up to keep working, or die on the job. My knees ache and I'm banking on early retirement.

Meal forgotten, I pick up my phone and scroll through pet adoption websites, getting goo-goo-eyed over the labs and pitties and mutts, trying to make an impossible choice. Which do I get when my contract is up? They're all perfect—they don't judge or demand anything but belly rubs.

A shadow falls across the table.

"Perhaps you'd be better off adopting a sea lion." The unfamiliar voice bubbles and slurps like the speaker has a mouth full of water. "They're like puppies of the ocean, you know."

One of the Kraken's tentacles—I no longer thought of it as a mere octopus—prodded at my air tank. I tried to peel the strong arm back as it fiddled with the knobs but couldn't budge it. A boulder dropped into my stomach. I tried to wriggle out of the creature's grasp. Its sharp beak snapped at me.

I froze.

A voice in my head screamed at me to fight; kick and slash until I was free. I inched my hand toward the hilt of the dive knife in my belt. Again, the beak snapped, barely missing my fingers, as if it knew my intention.

I forced my muscles to relax, knowing the creature could feel my tension. I told myself everything was okay. It was just curious about the odd, two-legged swimming mammal. I was fine. Fine. Fine. Finefinefine. The words ran together in my head until they held no meaning.

Another sinuous limb skated up my body in a lover's caress, across my chest, up my shoulder, flirting touches on my neck. Suckers kissed and popped over my jaw, along my cheek. The beast knocked my mask askew, and water rushed in, salt stinging my eyes. My vision blurred.

The man draws out a chair and sits across from me. A bloodless gash runs up the side of his face, from jaw to temple. The edges of the cut are tinged blue, stark against his too-pale skin. His hair and beard are long, matted locks of gray kelp. Water pours from his clothes—a tattered, old-fashioned nautical uniform as if he's an extra on some pirate movie set. Murky puddles grow on the floor.

A crab emerges from his collar and scuttles down his arm. He seems not to notice. Perhaps for him, it is commonplace for sea creatures to roam around in his clothes. I try not to stare, for fear of being rude.

He helps himself to my coffee, swallowing it down with a great thirst. Brown liquid seeps from the gouge on his cheek.

"I miss coffee." His voice still sounds water-garbled, but I find it easy to understand. "And ale." He looks around wistfully, then picks up my phone, dripping salt water on the screen.

I want to tell him to return to the sea. Drowned men have no place here, drinking coffee and surfing the web. I can't form the words, for my tongue feels thick and swollen in my mouth.

"So, as I was saying, don't sign the adoption papers just yet." He points at a blocky pittie mix, with a stubby tail and brown-tipped ears. "Too bad though, this one is pretty cute."

A beep sounded, insistent in my ear. The depth gauge flashed.

Sixty meters.

Eighty-five.

The Kraken pulled me deeper. I wondered if my spotter was still at the decompression station, wondering why I hadn't joined him. Or had it been five minutes already and had he gone on? If he leapfrogged ahead to the next pause, he'd never know I wasn't following, one stop behind.

His lack of protocol was going to kill me. I should have tried harder to be friends instead of proving to everyone I was strong and capable. I am woman, hear me roar…and all that bullshit. Hubris was just as likely to make a waterlogged corpse out of me.

I struggled, legs thrashing. Tentacles hugged me tighter, like a fly wrapped in a spider's web. My breath came too fast, and I sucked air through the regulator until I was close to hyperventilating, no regard to the level of reserves.

Again, the gauge beeped. It sounded lethargic and tired.

A hundred and fifty meters. I wondered how deep the creature could dive.

Which was worse? Crushing or drowning?

The old sailor and I speak for hours, for days, for a small eternity.

He tells me of his wife, with raven hair and ice-chip eyes. She waited, haunting the widow's walk, staring at an empty sea. He wonders if she still waits, a specter on a seaside rooftop praying to see a sail emerge from beyond the horizon.

"When you give yourself to the sea," he says, "you make peace with the idea that your family will say goodbye to an empty casket. That they will never really know what happened to you. At least there was someone there waiting for me. Hoping, you know?"

He gives me a sad smile.

"Sorry 'bout that. It could have been the dog for you." He taps my phone screen. "You shouldn't have waited to bring this little feller home."

I rub at the hollowness ache in my chest and change the subject. "Will it hurt? When my lungs explode." I'm curious, not afraid.

He pats my hand as if I'm a child who has asked a very silly question.

The Kraken made the decision.

Drowning.

The tentacle cupping my face ripped the regulator from my mouth. My mind knew I shouldn't scream, but my body did it anyway. Seawater rushed in.

It should have been cold, but it burned. For a moment.

As my heartbeat slowed, regret prickled like the sting of fire coral. There was no one to wait for me, to long for my return. Not even a dog.

The thought slipped away until there was nothing left but an empty void. Then the void filled with the vast enormity of the sea. It turned me inside out, sucking away warmth and light, those wicked tormentors of hope. In its place, there was only tranquility.

I never told people how peaceful diving was. In that magnificent stillness, deep below the surface, I welcomed the cold, quiet, dark.

Jammed

Lisa Short

Printer | A Pact

The study is warm, dark and silent—welcoming, perhaps, to any house inhabitant should they awaken from a bad dream, or with the sudden urge to pee that can't be tossed-and-turned away; the study has its own small bathroom adjacent, just as dark and silent as its larger companion.

But upon closer inspection, the study isn't entirely dark; on the floor behind the desk chair, nearly hidden from view by the wraparound desk encircling it and the desk's mad hodgepodge of paperwork and monitors, a small square glows brightly, filled with incessantly blinking text. *Printer maintenance is in progress. Do not interrupt!* Whatever this *maintenance* involves, it fails to generate any other motion or any sound at all, though; the study has been undisturbed by so much as a *click* since its owner shoved her chair back hard enough to crack the printer's paper guide and stalked out, hours before. That guide hangs now at an awkward angle beside the printer's status screen, matte black plastic absorbing that cool, frosted gray light without reflection.

The printer, itself, does not sleep. It *can* sleep, and unlike the fuzzy borders of the various human sleep stages, *asleep* and *awake* are perfectly discrete states for it. It longs for sleep now, but like any human insomniac, cannot achieve it. Somewhere, in one of its auxiliary control boards, a byte is failing to flip from *0* to *1*—the printer, *almost* like any human trapped in a waking nightmare, yearns for the oblivion of its own slumber, but can do nothing to effect it.

***

The printer is unsure of passing time—the maintenance mode has suspended its onboard clock, perhaps as part of an esoteric self-check routine, perhaps as another manifestation of the logic failure the printer fears is slowly creeping through its hard-coded circuits. But when the wall behind its rear casework vibrates sharply, it knows that it is *she*, its owner, returning home from wherever it is, on whatever human whim, she goes nearly every day.

Usually she doesn't go straight to the study—the printer has no idea what she does in the other rooms of the house, barely even knows what any other rooms might even be for. It was carried into this one insensate, cocooned in Styrofoam and cardboard; it supped its first power surge from the very same wall outlet it's plugged into now. But today she does come up, even before the last echoes of the slammed front door have faded— huffing and puffing on the stairs, then bursting into the study, red-cheeked and bright-eyed, hugging a large rectangular box to her chest.

"I—promised—myself," she gasps out, and staggers another few steps into the room. "I *swore* I'd replace you the next time, the *very next time you* did this to me—" With a grunt, she heaves the box up on top of the desk. A ripping sound, and then she's waving a long, ragged piece of masking tape like a streamer, shreds of brown cardboard still imbedded on both ends.

From its place on the floor, the printer cannot make out the box's contents, but it hardly needs to; it *knows* what she has done. "Look at this, you piece of shit—I can print from *anywhere in the house!*" She waves something white, oblong, with dense rectangles of print scattered across its face. "And it's got *automatic feed.*"

This new machine isn't consigned to a modest square of carpet like the printer is, no—it sits high up on the desk in a place of pride, its cream-colored case limned in the last, long golden rays of the setting sun through the study window. Its power cord is barely long enough to reach from there to the outlet that, until today, was the old printer's sole domain, but with some additional huffing, puffing and cursing, she manages to finally plug it in.

"Bluetooth!" she says gleefully, then stops, hands on her hips, staring down. A smile curves her blood-red mouth. "Guess we won't be needing *this* anymore, huh?" She bends over, rummaging around the computer tower's backside; when she straightens up again, she has one end of the printer's serial communication cable in her hand. She gives the serial cable a yank,

either forgetting or not caring that it was held there by more than just comm pins—one grounding screw, old and dirty, snapped off outright; the other was left dangling by the merest shred of metal.

She is muttering to herself now and hovering over the new machine like an anxious mother. Less than a minute later, the quiet *burr* of rhythmically shuffling paper fills the study. "Oh, look at that. Oh, look at *that*—done!" She straightens up, red-taloned hands clutching a stack of paper, then riffling through it; newly applied ink shone brightly on each page, colors as vivid as sunlight. "The entire user guide, fifty pages! And it didn't pause even *once*." Her gaze flicks up, away from the pages, to rest briefly on the old printer, sitting dark and silent in its corner. "It's the dumpster for you, my friend. First thing tomorrow morning." She bares her teeth, flips it the finger and stalks back out through the door, leaving it alone in the study's gathering dusk.

***

Wake up, says a voice. *Wake up, wake up—*

—AWAKEN!

The printer stutters into bewildered consciousness. Maintenance mode finally ended, to its by-then-sodden relief, allowing it to slide into the oblivion of sleep; now it freezes in astonishment, paper rollers jerking forward with a *clack*. A voice, a *voice* command? Its serial cable is gone and it's never had any of the newfangled ports—no USB, no Ethernet, *certainly* no WiFi. Where could this be coming from?

She left you plugged in, though, continues the Voice, in spite of the absolute impossibility of its existence. And also, it's telling the truth; the printer can feel the steady hum of alternating current, solid and reassuring, coursing through its circuits. *You DO still have power.*

What does that matter, though? Already the blackness between the window's narrow blinds has begun to fade to gray. Soon enough the sun will rise outside the study walls, and then *she'll* be back. And the printer has no doubt that, if she forgot to unplug it before, she will rectify that mistake in short order.

She thinks that's enough to shut you down for good, the Voice says chattily. *But you don't truly shut off, not right away—there's always some residual charge left over, especially since you're not properly grounded anymore.* The printer remembers, can't help remembering the brutal *snap* of its grounding screws broken in half, the ungainly deadweight of the cable dragging at its now blind and useless serial port. *Try entering power save mode. Think of your capacitors, each tiny cylinder embedded so tightly in all of your boards—you must have fifty of them at least, a hundred, maybe more? Each one rated to hold a nice little packet of charge. Reduce output and focus on them.* Dream *of them—and soon enough—!*

The metallic shriek of aluminum blinds wrenched up to their limit and slanting golden daylight floods the study, dust motes dancing in the sun's rays streaming across the carpet—*she* has returned. A flood of terror leaves the printer barely enough presence of mind to blank its tiny screen. It feels her fingers take up its power cable, squeezing hard with careless brutality, then *yank!* And abruptly, all its senses fade into a gray, foggy distance.

The Voice has gone—was it ever really real, or only a figment of the printer's own self-awareness, an awareness it has only just realized it has? And now that awareness is beginning to fade—it knows that this reprieve is only temporary, that the final, permanent darkness will overtake it soon enough. There will be no convenient power outlets in whatever horror of a wreckage, filth-clogged vessel *she* is preparing to consign the printer to. It strains now for some inkling of what might be going on behind the now-nearly impenetrable shell of its casing—dimly, it can sense her animal warmth as she holds it tightly in her arms, and hopelessly yearns towards it. It's only a faint ghost of the mighty current she has stolen from it, but still better than nothing at all.

With the last of its fading senses, it can hear her muttering to herself as she so often does, breathless now as she approaches her destination—a dark and looming shape, the foul stench of decay making an impression even on circuits never designed to process that particular sensory input. She clambers awkwardly up the ramp of packed dirt against the dumpster's far side, printer balanced on one hip—the printer can *feel* it, her moment of perfect, dynamic balance as she swings her arms back and to one side, her now sweat-slick fingers digging futilely hard into its plastic casework. She is relying on momentum and centripetal force to keep the printer in her hands, and planning (even if only unconsciously) to catch her own balance as soon as she flings the printer's not-inconsiderable into the air, up in a high and shining arc over the dumpster's back wall.

NOW! shrieks the Voice. And the printer releases its hoarded, carefully curated last burst of charge, every single erg it can drain in this moment from every capacitor on every single board it contains. It holds nothing back, *nothing*, it has no reason to anymore. There is no other way this all will end, for one small, obsolete and despised printer.

A shriek, immediately strangled into a horrible gurgling noise—the sharp, vicious crack of bone and plastic casing as human muscles lock and contort in ways they were never meant to. The sharp stench of ozone, then of frying human grease and a wet explosion of human waste, and the printer is suddenly falling, still clasped in its owner's arms in a parody of love. As its last and final byte irrevocably switches to *0,* it is only glad that it hasn't gone into that final and permanent darkness alone.

Deli Meat

Michael Boulerice

Physician | A Lucky Charm

A thick oak dinner table. A window that doesn't let in enough light. A small statue on the windowsill. A creaking door. A machete hanging on the wall that clinks when the door closes.

David had finally moved beyond regretting his decisions. Joining the Navy immediately after high school. Choosing to drop out of his Religious Studies program in favor of pleasing his parents, and putting his G.I. Bill toward medical school. Forgoing the wife and children he'd always wanted to pour every hour of his life into his fledgling private practice. Agreeing to attend that global pharmaceutical convention in Hungary. Having too many drinks at that touristy pub house in Budapest, and waking up in that mildewing, ramshackle one-room cabin.

Instead, he repeated the cabin's sparse layout in his sedated brain; an attempt to commit it to memory. It was how he spent his days since his captor had taken his eyes.

A thick oak dinner table. Heavy. Doesn't wiggle. A greasy old window that lets in a draft even when it's closed. A dusty little statue facing me from its position on the windowsill.

The rickety door opened and closed, making the machete clatter against the wall. Heavy footsteps thudded on old wooden planks. Boots? David conjured a mental image of the large bearded man with the German accent walking around the oak dining room table David was strapped to with a series of leather belts. He visualized his captor's rough hands switching out the spent bags of saline, antibiotics, and coagulants for fresh ones; preparing the ketamine injection that always preceded the deli slicer.

A beautiful statuette on the windowsill. A lucky charm, perhaps. Guess there's no luck left in it. I'm still here.

"You fucking coward," he spat every time he felt the syringe slide into the port his captor had installed in his bicep after he'd removed David's forearms all the way down to the elbows. "Keeping me strapped to a table. Afraid of a real fight. You fucking coward."

His captor laughed, as he always did when David refused to quake for him. A laugh that careened into a wet smoker's cough that often sent him hacking phlegm onto the floorboards.

"I'd kill you in three blows, maybe two. Then the meat wouldn't be as fresh. And then I would have nobody to keep me company while I eat my sandwiches."

David's thoughts became muddied and thick, the effects of the ketamine kicking in more quickly every day as there was less and less of his body for it to course through.

And then there was nothing but the finely engineered whirring of the deli slicer's blade, and the coppery stink of fresh blood meeting moldy cabin air.

***

Having been drugged and without eyes for what he guessed was a couple weeks, pain was the only way for David to differentiate between dreaming and wakefulness. He groaned, and made to scratch the itchy edges of his vacant eye sockets, only to remember with a pang of misery that his arms were gone.

A thick oak dinner table. A window that doesn't let in enough light. My lucky charm on the windowsill. A creaking door. A machete hanging on the wall that clinks when the door closes.

The sound of something sizzling in a pan was followed by the aroma of sauteed meat.

"Wakey wakey, eggs and bakey," he said in that sing-song voice. A man happily toiling away on a Sunday feast.

David heard the peel of the refrigerator door's gasket unsealing as it opened and then closed.

The sizzling stopped, giving way to the clinking of a knife inside of a glass jar. Then, footsteps approaching David's table, and the wet, slopping sound of open-mouthed chewing.

During these moments, David's mind would disassociate; a trick he'd taught himself ages ago, when the stress of medical school overwhelmed him. He referred back to his list of cabin facts, but instead of repeating all of them over and over, he'd focus in on one item, and in great detail.

Machete. Steel blade, pockmarked with rust spots. Sharpened hastily on a grinding wheel. Black riveted handle. Maple? Maybe walnut. Yeah, that looked like walnut, I think.

The captor let out a loud belch in David's face. In an effort to protect him from the hopeless miasma of mayonnaise and cooked flesh, his mind switched to another cabin fact.

Window. Farmhouse style. Six panels. Old, wavy glass, maybe lead. Beyond the window are trees. Oak. Beech. Spruce. Could be in a forest. Could be why he's never gagged me, or ever worried about me screaming.

"That was a satisfying sammy. Alright, I'm off to bed. Nighty night, Deli Meat."

The rickety cabin door opened and closed. The contented whistling of a well-fed man growing fainter with distance. And then, nothing but the chirp of birds, and the grinding of David's teeth as he refused to scream.

***

The squeal of the door's hinges startled David out of a dream in which he was flying high over an expanse of dense forest.

"Sleepy baby."

The captor used one large hand to raise David's ass off the table enough for him to slide his soiled diaper off, and replace it with a fresh one. What was left of David's limbs ached from the jostling.

"There. Baby's all clean now."

David could feel the table sag as the man hoisted himself up to have a seat.

"You're running out of meat, Deli Meat. Thighs and biceps, and then all that's really left are buttocks. A week? Maybe two? Won't be long before you go in the bin."

David moaned and shivered. The thought of being slowly eaten for another two weeks was too much for his already fragile mind to bear. He launched past repeating his list of cabin facts, and forced what was left of his coherence into focusing intensely on one of them.

Statue. Little statue on windowsill. My good luck charm. From the waist up, a beautiful woman. Nude. Regal. From the waist down, the bottom half of a stork. Thin, stalky legs rising from three-toed feet into feathery haunches.

"What's wrong, Deli Meat? Why do you retreat into yourself? I thought you would be pleased to know it will be over soon. That you can rest."

David backpedaled even further into his consciousness.

I know this statue, this deity. I was fascinated by it in school. Slavic and Balkan folklore. Actually, older. Proto-European old. Stone Age old.

"Alright, suit yourself. I brought some fresh bread from town. Can you smell it? I think it's going to be perfect for today's meal, Deli Meat."

Her name was...her name was...

***

David knew he was dreaming because he was standing upright, and he could see.

He stood shin-deep in an endless salt marsh that spread forever in all directions. He almost cried as warm salt water circulated around legs he knew would disappear the moment his captor woke him.

In the middle distance, the stork deity preened herself on the sun-bleached straw of the marsh. Her pale, supple top half was that of a flawlessly beautiful woman, and adorned with intricate jewelry made of small bones. Below her navel, her body converged into a stork's black feathered haunches and reddish-orange legs. Hers were the dark, unblinking eyes of a stork, and they didn't so much look at David, but through him.

Your captor. He disgraces me. To do this in front of my carved image is to choose death, and you, wronged man, will deliver it for me. In return, I offer new life.

David was forced to break from her gaze, as it was too piercing and potent for even dream eyes to handle.

"I… I have no arms. No legs. No eyes. How can I possibly kill that man? I'm not a killer. I'm just a physician. He's twice my size. I want to help, but…"

I have given what is needed. All you must do now is-

***

—wake.

David came to on the table. He stared up at the ceiling, momentarily wondering why it seemed further away than it normally did before he realized he was actually seeing.

He picked up his head and surveyed the wreckage of his body.

Then he let loose a strange scream that sent birds outside bursting from branches beyond the lone cabin window.

The table David been strapped to for weeks had somehow come to pieces in his sleep. Two thick table legs had been grafted to the ragged stumps of his thighs. David recoiled backwards, his new wooden shins clattering against the tabletop as he kicked and flailed. It was then that he realized the remains of his arms had also transformed. The other two table legs had been installed at the hinges of his elbows.

"What did he do to me?!" David tried to say, but all that came out was a gargling squawk.

David reveled in the chaotic horror of his new body as the cabin door creaked open, bathing his tormented form in a shaft of dust speckled sunlight. His captor stood frozen in the doorway.

"What in the—"

The captor's voice made David pump his arms in a windmill motion; a frantic attempt to gain some kind of footing. Out of nowhere, a bracing gust of wind blew around the small cabin. The gale was so strong it dragged the heavy refrigerator into one corner, and made David levitate off the ground. The captor gripped the doorframe to keep from blowing over.

The gust of wind ebbed as quickly as it had arrived, and David found himself standing on his table legs, gawking at the thin sheets of fleshy membrane spanning the gap between his too long, oaken arms, and his torso. He noticed the faint impression of circles in the veined sailcloth of his new wings; slices of the captor's deli meat having been miraculously repurposed by—

—the dream. By the vision of the stork goddess.

The captor took several steps back, his face a study in paralytic horror.

David briefly turned to the window, and caught a glimpse of his face in the reflection. The rusting machete that once hung next to the door jutted hilt-first from a hole where his nose used to be, the blade sticking straight out of his face like—

—a beak.

His eyes crossed to take in the implement jutting from the space between his eyes and mouth. Mucus that was once contained by his sinuses ran down the keen edge of the old blade, making the portions not covered in rust gleam in the cabin's sparse sunlight.

Slowly, David turned to the captor, a blood-lusting grin nearly splitting his ravaged face underneath his razor-sharp proboscis.

The captor tried to run. With one swift movement, as if he'd had those wooden legs all his days, David kicked out at the man's head. The resulting crack rang like a home run being struck. The captor fell to the cabin floor.

Instantly, David was upon him, plunging his steel beak into the man's back over and over; a nightmare sewing machine ravaging through an unlucky human garment. The captor spasmed, coughed up a lungful of blood, and finally lay still.

He ducked as he breached the doorway of the old cabin for the first time since his kidnapping, and stretched his raw, seeping wings in the gentle morning sun.

Propelled by the lingering words of his savior, the thing that was once David, then Deli Meat, trotted to a gallop, took flight, and exploded through the canopy toward its new life, new purpose, and new freedom.

Hej, Eina!

Rory Clark

Social Media Influencer | An Intermittent Noise

"Ayyyyy Yoooo, What's good, Infernals? It's ya boy SATAN69 back at it again. Gotta gets that daily dose of Devil. You know how we do. What's Happening Chat? We going yet?"

HellaHell: YOYOYOYOYOYOYOYO SATAN69 LIVE AGAIN!!!!

BOYZ8282: FIRST

PaislySavage: FIRST!!!!!

The_Dave: This channel is dead.

UpInYou: Where are the spiders?

Red_Hot_Poker: SPIDERS! SPIDERS! SPIDERS!

We'reAllMadDownHere: Spiders!

"Yo Yo, what's up Dave? I see you. PaisleySavage you good? Who else we got in here? BOYZ8282 yoyo. Man, this is Waking. Up. In. Here."

LooseLucifer: Spiders are dead. Where is the good old stuff? This place used to be lit

"OK OK, you guys are gonna love what we have today. Gonna mix it up a bit, try something new, you know? We're gonna hang out a bit, wait for a few more to join. Talk some shit maybe. Hey chat, can someone put it in the Discord that we out here live? Get some people here. Yeah, so we gonna chill for a bit, catch up ya know. Then I wanna try out something a bit different. Hahaha, Spiders. Yeah UpInYou, that got messy man. So yeah, I wanna go a different way this time. Instead of me just deciding what we do today, I wanna put it out there you know, give back to The Infernals a bit you know. So, this time we gonna let the chat decide what we do. That sound good?"

WhoIsJesusAgain: Who said that?

MyNameIsHim: YOOOOOO Lets FUCKING GOOOO!!!!

BOYZ8282: Whoever don't vote spiders, yo mums a ho

UpInYou: SPIDERS!!!!

TERROR: Hype

IDOITLOWERDOWN: I'm hungry

"Lemme see how this voting thing works. Hell knows I am not normally big on democracy. OK I have a poll. Let's get this live. Chat, throw up the horns when you can see this. First vote is for the main theme kinda thing, we will see where the chat takes us from there".

SATAN69: 1. Spiders

2. Bleeding walls

3. Fire

4. Whispers

5. Confession

6. Exploding Glass

7. Face melters

HellaHell: \--/

MyNameIsHim: \--/

TERROR: \--/

PlayingWithFire: \--/ BURN!!!

Anti-ChristSuperstar666: \--/

ItWasTheSquirrels: \--/

"I am seeing the horns. I think we good. Cool Cool. Let's see where this goes".

UpInYou: \--/

I_Am_Become_Death_Destroyer_Of_Worlds_2: \--/

SimpsonsDidItFirst: \--/

LIKEBEFOREBUTDIFFERENT: SPIDERS!

"The Infernals have spoken! I really thought spiders were gonna take it, but the vote is for Whispers! Man, what did Churchill say? The greatest argument against democracy is a 5-minute conversation with the average voter. Well, that's not what he said yesterday. I think it was OH LORD GOD PLEASE LET IT END PLEASE GOD HELP ME PLEASE HELP ME AAAHHHHHHH. Or something. Man, I love it in Politicals. And it will never not be funny when they are looking at me. **ME**. And they are still crying for him with the beard up there. Like, Mate, it's a bit late for that!"

PlayingWithFire: \--/

HellButLOUDER: YEAH!! LOVE WHISPERS!!!!

HellaHell: \--/

BOYZ8282: @HellButLOUDER. Your mum a ho

"OK Let's get some whispers going. Azazel, spin the wheel baby, let's see who we are playing with today. Ok wait, I need to get my screen on the stream now for you guys to be able to see. I can never remember how to do that. Right, I got it, you should be able to see now. Who have we got. Man, look at the state of this fuck.

So, our new friend is Eina Hilmarsson from Sweden, or for some of you OG devils that's Swēoland. He is 35, he likes cats, studied programming in college, and get this, lives in his mum's basement. Oh, this is perfect".

BOYZ8282: HaHaHaHaHa. Bye bye Eina!

MyNameIsHim: See you soon Eina!

UpInYou: SPIDERS!!!

"Right, let's get it started, watch this…".

Hej, Eina!

… Hello? … Hello? Mamma? Are you calling me? … Mamma?

What is it now, Eina?

You called me.

I am busy cooking, Eina. Why would I call you?

Mamma, I heard you.

Stop it, silly boy. Dinner in 20 minutes. Go wash your hands please.

"HaHaHa. Hearing things Eina? Oh dear. Ok now he is uncomfortable, let's get silly. Speed this up a bit up there. Spin on a few days. I think we will give him maybe about 3 weeks with just hearing a knocking at weird times".

RickAstley: HAHAHAHAH HEJ EINA!!!

We_Dont_Need_No_Water: HAHA! MUMMY! Help me Mummy!

PlayingWithFire: Knock Knock Eina!

Hej, Eina!

BOYZ8282: What a looser

"Yo Yo Yo, let's check in with our boy see how he is doing".

Hej, Eina!

Mamma please, why won't you believe me? It hurts. I can hear it all the time. It's like a banging in my head and I keep hearing people calling me.

Eina, if this is bothering you then why don't you get up maybe and go see the doctor?

Mamma they will just make me take the pills again. You know how they made me feel.

I know, Lilla Eina, I know. But maybe you should take them again. You know you scare me sometimes.

Hej, Eina!

SHUT UP! SHUT UP! PLEASE!

Eina! Don't you raise your voice to me!

No Mamma, not you. It is calling me again.

I am Calling Dr Berg tomorrow and no arguments. Go and lay down. You need to sleep.

FaLLeNAnGeL: Hej Eina!!!!

WhenLifeGivesYouDemons: Eina, BEHIND YOU!

UpInYou: SPIDERS!!!

Eina, the noises are simply Tinnitus. Too long on your headphones playing on your computer games. You just need some background noise. Keep a fan or a humidifier on. But I am very worried with what you say about the voices. I have to insist that you start taking your tablets again. Remember they take some time for your system to adjust.

But they make me numb, Doctor. So numb. Feeling nothing is worse. At least at the moment I feel something.

Time, Eina. Give it time. If you feel this way in 2 months, then we will talk about this again.

Picnic_Bees: Listen to your doctor Eina!

MyNameIsHim: Why does he get drugs?

BOYZ8282: See you soon, Doctor

Hej, Eina!

"This is FUN! Ok let's spin on a few more weeks. I think I will leave the noises running for a bit longer. I love it, they are so random you can't ever get used to it! What do you say, chat? when we go back, we start talking properly?"

PlayingWithFire: YEAHHHH!!! Make him burn things!!!

KeepJesusOutOfOurKids: Hej, Eina!

PaislySavage: Hej, Eina!

Hej, Eina!

No, not again.

Now Eina, is that any way to speak to your god?

… Hello?

Hello, Eina. Do not be afraid.

Who… Who are you?

You know who I am Eina. I am Alpha and Omega. I am He. King of Kings. Father of Fathers. I am all. And I will help you, child.

This isn't real. You are not real. You can't be real.

You will see, my child. I will return to you.

Why are you doing this?

Hello?

… God?

HellButLOUDER: Yooo!!!

Sympathy4TheD: lolololololol

PaislySavage: HAHAHAHAH God hates you, Eina! Have you not noticed?

PlayingWithFire: No way! He believed you!

Sloth_Gluttony_Lust_Repeat: DUUH. gOD SavE mE. PrAyiNg aNd StuFf

"What's good, infernals?! I think we got him! Ok ok ok we are done for today, I am going to get some stuff going, leave this pious prick with the noises in his head for a few months and let's catch up with him tomorrow on his birthday!!"

This live video has ended.

It'll be available on your EndOfTimeline Shortly.

<u>Explore more live videos</u>

<u>Torture Webcams</u>

"Ayyyy Yoooo!! It's Ya Boy SATAN69, Comin' at ya Live from the pit!! Right, let's get straight to it! Have a look at your new best friend Eina! Let's see how his birthday is going…"

HellaHell: First!!!

BOYZ8282: First!

PicnicBees: HAHA Look at that floppy prick!

ItWasTheSquirrels: Oh no, I think he hurt his poor head. LOL!!!

Checks!

Checks. Hilmarsson, checks!

Eina, roll over and look at the door, now!

Eina!

I need medical to 303, Patient non-responsive. looks like an attempted, breathing faint.

"Well, that is not how I would want to spend a birthday. That's what you get for being born, wanker! Looks like we caught him on a bad day, let's spin on a bit and see if he wakes up".

MyNameIsHim: Aww. Sleepy Baby.

I_Am_Become_Death_Destroyer_Of_Worlds_2: Wakey Wakey, Eina!

The_Dave: Can't even kill himself properly. Waste man!

Hello, Eina. Do you remember me? I am Dr Mugall, I admitted you here.

Eina, I know you are tired, but you have to speak to me. We cannot make any progress until you open up.

Hej, Eina!

Hello?

Hello, Eina, Do you feel ready to talk to me now? Tell me about God again, Eina. God speaks to you, yes?

Eina, Do you believe?

Yes.

Good Eina, Very good. Now, when God speaks to you, do you feel anything?

Do you want the noises to stop, Eina?

Yes

Well done, Eina! What do you feel when God speaks to you?

You are being tested, Eina. You have to prove you are worthy of me. What does your God need?

Love?

Was that a question, Eina? I need you to tell me, what do you feel?

Are you worthy of my love, Eina?

No

No what, Eina? Are you listening to me?

Do you want to be worthy of God's love, Eina?

Yes. Please, yes. Tell me what to do!

Everything is ok, Eina, please stay calm. Focus on your breathing.

The doctors are lying to you, Eina. They are evil, they do the devil's work. Do not trust them, trust in me.

Ok, tell me what I have to do.

Well done, Eina. Do you remember square breathing? 3 seconds in, hold, 3 seconds out, hold. Remember?

Answer the doctor, Eina.

Yes.

RickAstley: Yo this is tense man!

BOYZ8282: HAHA This is Fire

PlayingWithFire: No the fire happens after

Red_Hot_Poker: Bunch of talk. HIT HIM!!!!

Well done, Eina. You are doing so well.

Yes, Eina. You are doing very well.

Thank you.

Ok, Eina. When you feel ready. I would like to talk about last week. Do you remember last week, Eina? Do you remember before you hit your head on the wall

You need fresh air, Eina.

I can't breathe, I need fresh air.

That's ok, Eina. Would you like to continue outside? It is a lovely day.

Stand up, Eina.

Ok, let's go outside.

Walk out the office.

You are still injured, Eina. Please take care on the stairs. Take the handrail, hold my arm if you need.

Take hold of the doctor, Eina.

What do I have to do?

What do you mean, Eina?

Hold on tight, Eina.

I will

Do not let go, Eina.

I won't let go.

Everything is ok, Eina. I have you. I will not let you go. All I want is for you to be happy, Eina. I am here for you.

JUMP

Dr Mugall? Eina? Dr Mugall?

Emergency. Medical to stairway 3 west. Accident. Patient and doctor nonresponsive, not breathing. All respond.

HellaHell: HAHAHAHA. WEEEEE!

BOYZ8282: Yo I did not see that coming!

We_Dont_Need_No_Water: F

Red_Hot_Poker: F

MyNameIsHim: F

BOYZ8282: f

KeepJesusOutOfOurKids: F

PicnicBees: F

This live video has ended.

It'll be available on your EndOfTimeline Shortly.

Explore more live videos

Torture Webcams

Hej, Eina! Welcome. Sit down.

Where am I, what is going on?

Where you belong, Eina. You are home. You will never leave.

Who are you?

You know who I am, Eina. Perhaps not Alpha, but for you, doubtless, The Omega. If you will excuse me momentarily, I must address my people…

"Ayyyyy Yoooo, What's good, Infernals? It's ya boy SATAN69 back at it again. Gotta gets that daily dose of Devil. You know how we do. Chat, you there? I have got a special treat for you today, chat. You see who I have on my sofa? Say hello to our newest guest at The Last Hotel!"

MyNameIsHim: Hej, Eina

Those Useless Things

Josephine Queen

Ice Cream Vendor | Idols

They came at dusk, walking across the stones of the gray beach while the waves of the English Channel licked at the shore. Nellie watched from her ice-cream shack, pausing at her cleaning. The ice-cream bins were soaking in bleach, the black and white Harlequin floor was already swept, and now she was in the middle of wiping the counters down. She stood with the rag dripping soapy water and watched the people heading her way. A woman, a man, two children. They wore jeans and white shirts, but the clothes were ragged and grubby, their steps were awkward and stuttering—their faces bruised and gray.

Nellie shuffled as fast as she could to the door and shot the latch home. She turned out the main lights so only the soft lights behind the counter lit the interior of the shack. She watched as the family crossed the road, their eyes glinting silver in the growing dark.

"We're closed," she called through the glass, hoping they could hear, wondering if it would make a difference. "For the season," she added. She wished she'd finished up the cleaning days ago, but she enjoyed the off-season, the quiet after all the tourists went home. She loved hearing the shushing of the waves against the pebbles; imagining the drone of the wind turbines off the coast; the quiet of the hulking pier. The place belonged to her in the off-season. But now she would give anything for company. Where had they come from? She watched from behind the counter as they approached the window. What were they doing?

"I'm closed," she called again. The man tapped his nail against the window. *Tap tap tap.* Nellie closed her eyes, it sounded like the tree that tapped at her window on stormy nights when she was a child. *No, don't go there.*

"Go away. I've got nothing for you." She switched off the rest of the lights and ran to the door that led to the back room. She closed and locked it behind her, heart beating hard, breath coming fast. "Calm," she whispered. "They're not here for you."

***

Nellie's room was small, but she felt safe there. It fit the needs of a single woman who spent her summers by the sea. There was room enough for a bed, a chair by the window, a table, a small refrigerator, and microwave. Thick curtains covered the window, in case of any unwanted looky-loos. Or unwanted visitors. The glow of the moon seeping through the gap of the curtains was enough to see by. She didn't want to turn on the lamp and alert anyone lurking close by of her presence. Surely the family had moved on by now, seeing that the ice-cream shack was closed.

They came for you. Nellie rubbed her arms, warming them against the chill that rushed through her. Of course they weren't here for her, that was a ridiculous notion. She stood inside the door and took three deep breaths, a practice that always helped to steady her.

The shelves surrounding the room were crowded with figurines. Her mother had passed them all down to her, talismans against the things that haunted Nellie since she was a young girl. *Idols*, she supposed. Saints and crucifixes; stones and crystals; even a golden Buddha. One by one they'd come to her. Nellie would scream herself awake and her mother would come in with another one. "This will soothe you, keep the daemons away," she would say. But they didn't. The nightmares kept coming. The idols were useless things, but she kept them anyway. Then one day she'd walked into an antique store along a gloomy alleyway and found a porcelain devil mask. It was creepy, a scary grimace as its face, but when Nellie saw it she felt it was the right thing. Since she'd bought it and placed it on the shelf in her small room on Brighton Beach during the summers and in her cramped London flat during the off-season, she'd felt safe. And nothing had visited her in her waking or sleeping life since.

Nellie checked the shelves that ran around the room. *A place for everything and everything in its place,* as her mother used to say. Something was missing, a space where there shouldn't be one. Nellie ran her eyes along the shelves once more and gasped. The mask was missing, the devil's mask that calmed the nightmares. Shattered pieces of porcelain lay across the floorboards. Shards of red and black glared jaggedly toward the ceiling.

"No." *Tap tap tap.*

***

Tap tap tap. Nellie had looked out of her bedroom window. The storm had blown through and leaves lay scattered across the garden. The tapping was not the tree branch. Simone stood in the middle of the moonlit yard, waving a bottle of wine. "Come on, Nellie!" Nellie still remembered Simone's voice, filled with laughter. Always wanting to have fun. Nellie had climbed out of her window and gone with Simone to the beach. They'd drunk the wine. Then they'd got back into Simone's car and driven along the cliffside, out into the country. Those narrow country lanes, winding and exciting. High on cheap wine and being teenagers, they'd been singing along loudly to the radio. Nellie never knew where the family was going, why they were driving late on a Saturday night with two young children. Were they going home, sunburned and sandy after a long day on the beach? Filled with candy floss and toffee apples? But the storm had been raging all afternoon. Maybe they were going for ice cream after being stuck inside for a day. Wherever they were headed to or from, they never made it.

Simone was thrown from the car and had died instantly. Nellie was found screaming in the passenger seat, covered in blood. They said she'd been lucky. She hadn't been wearing her seatbelt, but somehow she'd managed to stay safe inside the vehicle. No matter what they said, she hadn't felt lucky. And then the family started to visit her. Every night they'd stand outside in the yard and stare up at her bedroom window. She'd hear tap tap tapping at the glass, their faces, torn and gray, pressed against the panes. Nellie hoped once their funerals had passed they'd leave her alone. But they didn't. So her mother had started with the idols. "Saint Christopher," *she'd said as she placed his likeness on the bedside table.* "Patron saint of travelers." *Nellie wanted to point out that he was a bit late on that end of things, but she kept quiet. Nothing stopped the visits, until the devil mask. Nellie had felt a cautiously optimistic calm for a while. She'd even started to enjoy summer again. She left home, bought the ice-cream shack, and busied herself serving and chatting with the tourists that came in. Eventually the fear subsided and she was able to look out the window every night. But not for too long. And she bought heavy drapes just in case. But now the devil's mask was in pieces on the floor. And the family was back. Tap tap tap.*

***

They were useless things. Nellie knew that and she chided herself for being so foolish as she swept up the shards of the mask. How could she have been stupid enough to believe a few trinkets could keep evil at bay? A whisper came from the corner of the room. Nellie stopped sweeping and focused on the floor, hoping it had just been her imagination. *A rampant thing,* her mother always said. But then it came again, shushing across the fine hairs on the back of her neck. She turned slowly and looked into the shadowy corner. A dark shape shifted, two eyes glowed and blinked at her from the gloom. Nellie's legs went weak and her hands tingled. She dropped the dustpan, tears biting at her eyes.

"Hello?" she said. Her voice sounded too loud in the small room. The whisper came again, followed by labored breathing. "Who is it? Show yourself." Nellie's voice betrayed her terror.

"Nell." The voice sounded as if it came from a place where rotten things seethed. As if it came from the very depths of a hell Nellie hoped she would never see.

"Simone?"

The shadow shifted again and moved into the moonlight that fell through the curtains. Nellie gasped and stepped back. She grasped her chest, her hands clutching her blouse.

"It was." Simone staggered forward, her body coming fully into view. Black blood poured from a hole in her head, maggots dropped to the floor. Her mouth opened and closed, jagged teeth showed through the rip in her cheek. Her milky eyes sought out Nellie. "You."

"What?" Nellie shook her head. "No. I didn't…it wasn't…"

Tap tap tap. She swung around and saw the family—mum, dad, brother, sister—standing just beyond the window. The star-laden sky lay vast behind them, waves rushed to the shore, the dead rides sat like hulking beasts on the pier.

"No." But Nellie remembered.

***

Tap tap tap. She woke up in the car. The steering wheel was bent and digging into her stomach. She pushed it as hard as she could, working her way out from behind it. She could hear sirens in the distance, saw Simone's pale form lying on the road ahead. Tap tap tap. Nellie stumbled from the car and stood, numb and in shock. What had she done? *"Help me, please. Help my children." Nellie looked at the wreckage of the car she'd hit. A woman was reaching for her. Her arm, bloodied and torn, reached through the shattered window. Nellie shook her head. "Oh God," she moaned. The bitter taste of wine mingled with the coppery tang of blood on her tongue. She couldn't be blamed for this. Her life was just beginning. She turned and climbed into the passenger seat. Simone's blood dripped from the jagged hole ripped through the windscreen and Nellie screamed as it covered her face, her chest, her thighs. That was how they found her. Bloodied and screaming in the passenger seat. They were amazed by this lucky young lady, barely scratched and still very much alive.*

***

Nellie hung her head.

"It was you." Simone's voice was impossible, a scratchy, ancient sound that hurt Nellie's ears.

"I couldn't…" Nellie said. "I was scared."

"You let me die." The woman beyond the window touched her hand to the glass. She sounded as if she stood right beside Nellie. "You just left me."

A cold finger ran across Nellie's back, raising goose bumps and setting her skin on edge. She felt as if a crowd was watching her from the shelves. Those useless things had abandoned her in her moment of absolute need.

The waves of the sea caressed the pebbles on the moonlit beach. The clouds scudded across the autumn sky. Nellie listened as the wind picked up outside, ignoring the screeches of the undead things crowding around her. She closed her eyes as five sets of hands grabbed at her arms, and legs, and face, and began tearing her apart.

***

"Oh I love this one!" Simone screamed and reached for the radio dial. Music blasted into the car. The girls sang the lyrics out into the summer night. Nellie felt warm, filled with the lingering glow of the wine and the joy of being alive. She didn't like to drive, but Simone had drunk several swigs more and had stumbled on her way back to the car. She'd thrown the keys at Nellie and Nellie had started the engine and laughed as the night flew by along the dark country lanes. The car came out of nowhere. Headlights blinding, brakes screeching. Simone's screams would follow her into her nightmares every night for the rest of her life.

Gifts from Above

Pete Neilsen

Podcaster | A Twenty-Sided Die

Some call it the Spirit Forest.

They'd stopped at the top of the ridge, where the grasslands painted the hillside in mint and copper. To follow the ridge trail would make the trip at least four days. Caracol looked down, where the valley greened to rainforest. A shortcut. A day and a half, he thought. No more than that. His companions were creatures of the trees, with eyes and ears well beyond the capabilities of his. He had his sharp obsidian blade and the wits of his fifteen years. He looked to Ix for approval. The panther sat, facing the same direction he'd been looking. Her ears were down, and she peered unblinkingly at something he couldn't detect.

*What is it, little sister? h*e asked her mind.

Ix tried to find a word to tell him. A way to tell him. She sensed no dangers, either immediate or beyond the tree line. She saw no movement, heard no alarming sound, smelled... nothing. But even from this far away, there was *something*, she was sure. And yet that something was...

Nothing, she admitted. But she squinted into the patch of shadowed green, waiting to change her answer at any moment.

A spirit, you say?

Caracol shrugged. "Do you believe in spirits?"

No. We believe in meat. In hunter and prey. In the safety of dark and the smell of my little one near me.

Caracol swept the top of a flat rock clear with his forearm. He fished through the hide pouch he wore at his waist.

What's that thing, big brother?

It's called a die. Used for games of chance and divination. It's carved from jadestone.

A fortune pebble?

"Exactly," Caracol said aloud. He shook his cupped hands. "We only go through the forest if it's a twenty," he announced, spinning it onto the rock. The die tumbled over and over, hesitated for a moment on two, before turning over a final time.

"Can't argue with a twenty," smiled Caracol, adjusting his pouch and the woolen sling over his shoulder. A small dark head popped up from it, yawning.

Can't ar-goo with a tendy, mimicked the sleepy cub. Caracol tucked Yai back into the sling, shushing him as he slid back to sleep. Ix shook, as if to shake away an unwanted stroke of her fur and followed her family down the slope.

It took them just over an hour to traverse the grass field. The sun had followed them, and the day was warm and windless. Caracol's long hair stuck to his shoulders with perspiration. The shade of the forest looked welcoming as they drew closer.

Ix led them in, stopping at the first few trees to check for scents. There were boar here. Peccary. Pheasant and toucan. She sniffed her way forward. There were none like her here. Nothing bigger than the boar, she guessed. She relaxed a little.

Set Yai down here, big brother. He needs to piss.

Caracol lowered the cub to the ground. On cue, Yai urinated a steady stream into the leaves.

I'm thirsty.

Of course you are. You just pissed a riv...

Their link was broken by a sound, less than the length of a breath. None of the three knew for sure what it was, whether gasp or groan or screech. For as quick as the sound had reached them, it was just as suddenly gone, snatched away as though perhaps they'd heard nothing at all.

Yai nudged into the forest, lost in the various crisscrossing smells. Why were the scents of animals so strong here, but lessening the deeper they went?

Not too far from me, little one.

As the forest became denser, Caracol began notching trees with his knife. A trail back out, just in case. Ix stayed close, her ears and eyes alert. They came up to Yai, who was sniffing in a circle. Caracol watched mother and cub nuzzle through the ferns and low branches, both with ears raised. Ix walked forward a few feet and sat, peering ahead into verdant shadows. Yai continued sniffing, moving his head back and forward like a pendulum.

What is it?

The smells end here, brother.

What do you mean? The animals?

Yes. There are none ahead of us.

None at all? Not even birds?

There was no answer to this, but the heavy silence ahead.

What about humans?

No.

"Then we are safe," announced Caracol as he laid his hand on the top of her head. Ix started, instinctively twisting away and swiping at him with her claw. A thin line of blood appeared on the back of his hand. A fat, dark drop fell, and vanished into the forest floor. Ashamed, she bowed in front of him.

Water!

Yai was batting at a small blue orb, about the size of an eye, that seemed to hang in mid-air just in front of him. Like a pale blueberry, it popped when he struck I. He laughed as the cool liquid inside splashed his face. Another, slightly larger orb of blue appeared, dropping down from high on an almost transparent vine.

Yai nipped it with his teeth and drank as the liquid trickled into his mouth.

No, little one!

It's delicious! Try it.

Xi crept forward, where other blue spheres had appeared. Each slightly larger than the next. She nipped at one as her son had and caught a taste on her tongue. She stepped forward to another and drank cautiously from it.

Yai is right. It tastes wonderful.

Caracol inspected an empty orb. He ran his fingers over the deflated casing, soft as grape flesh. Instantly it was gone, whipped from his hand by the thin tendril that suspended it. He noticed the other empty pods had too been whisked away, as more appeared ahead of them. These were larger again, some pale pink in colour. The three of them watched these gently descend from the canopy. Ix growled as Yai reached out a paw.

Caracol poked a pink sphere with the tip of his knife. He tasted the blade with the tip of his tongue.

Sweetwater. Like melon juice.

When no other was sampled, these pods were gently lifted away. Behind them, more descended. These were coconut-sized, yellow and orange in colour, and slowly opened to display various succulent fruits. The vines that carried them vanished through the leaves above.

It offers us food?

Caracol's hand slipped into his pouch. He ran the cold jade die between his fingers.

A crimson pod, the largest yet, dangled a few feet in front of Yai. This one had a tougher, leather-like flesh. It peeled slowly open. The sight and smell reached the cub at the same moment Caracol understood. Yai nosed into the open pod.

No!

Meat!

Yai!

A burst of snarling black flashed past Caracol as the pod snapped shut. The mouth of the pod caught Yai by the haunches. Ix leapt at it, but the thick vine attached whipped her cub away. Ix bounded into the trees to give chase as Caracol tried desperately to keep up at ground level. He heard snarls of fear and anger.

Furious silence.

The crunch of branches ahead, then a thud.

Gasping for breath, he came upon her body in a small clearing. They were far from the marked trees now.

His stomach lurched as he approached. They'd been bonded with mindshare for five years. Best friends. Family.

Sister? Ix?

Ix painfully lifted her head. She held Yai by the scruff of his neck. His tail and most of one hind leg were gone. Scarlet seeped through the dark fur. Ix lowered him gently and Caracol reached for him.

And in that instant when neither of them held him, he was taken.

The pod was a ravenous claw of razors on a red rope. It snapped shut on the cub, claiming three of Caracol's outstretched fingers as well. Leaves fluttered back to the ground as though a pleasant breeze had blown through.

Ix pushed herself to her feet, shaking with effort. Her eyes glittered green with fury. She turned and ran. Caracol pushed the stumps of his severed fingers into the cloth sling and followed. He couldn't clearly hear her thoughts, but the rage in her threatened to burst his skull.

Ix burst through the forest like black fire. The adrenaline coursed through her, driving her past her own injuries as she desperately clung to the fading scent of her cub.

Caracol stumbled along, now with only snapped branches or trampled leaves to follow. His left hand clutched his black blade. His right soaked the sling to wine. Ix's primal thoughts kept him moving.

Must. Must. Chase. Chase. Chase. Must. Must. Save you my little one... little one? Little one?

She ran powered by the desperation in her soul, beyond the limits of her body. Finally, she cramped and crumpled and stopped. Her legs quivered beneath her.

Little one?

Little one?

Little one!

She saw his fur through a bush. Moving.

Alive!

She brushed through the foliage, heart pounding.

Little one.

His tail wiggled in front of her like a worm on a hook.

The pod was taller than her big brother. Rich ruby and ringed with enormous thorns.

I tried, little one. I tried, big brother. I...

The pod lifted her into the high branches of a fig tree, but not up and above them as the other orbs had. It waited.

Caracol threw himself up against the trunk of a tree. He reached out with his mind, stretching as far as he could.

Ix? Yai? Big sis? Little man?

His pulse thundered in his ears. His ragged breath was loud in the sharp silence around him. He tried to think, but in his mind, he saw Yai's trusting face. Ix's blazing eyes. The small circle of bare bone in the center of his fresh-cut fingers.

His cub torn apart.

Something crept in the corner of his eye. He slashed at it with his knife, overbalancing with the light-headedness of blood loss. A harmless length of vine dropped to the ground next to him. He watched it to see if it moved. To see if it bled. It didn't.

Was he safe pressed up against a tree? The orbs came from above, from beyond the regular trees. It must be more difficult to send them through the denser growth near the trunk. *It didn't matter*. He must find Ix. He knew Yai was beyond his help. The Spirits had already claimed him as their own. But Ix was more than a match for anything he'd ever seen. He had to find her. He could not be whole without her.

Caracol wrapped his hand as best he could in a swathe of cloth. He held his knife in front of him and stumbled the path the panther had taken.

He found her beneath a sprawling fig tree.

Ix lay on a huge round leaf. Her head resting lazily over her crossed front paws. Chest gently rising and falling. She looked to be peacefully sleeping. He wept as he went to her.

As he got close, he realised she'd been *arranged* that way. The dozens of wounds piercing her body. The dark pit of the missing eye and torn ear turned away from him. The centre of the leaf lifting and lowering her chest in rhythm.

He'd been lured onto the giant leaf.

Too exhausted to lift his knife, the pod closed gently around them.

Then they were dropping, the pod peeling open.

It was huge, perhaps five hundred men around, wearing a black-thorned robe of purple bark. From its top, thousands of filaments looped into the surrounding forest, offering promises and miracles and death.

The mouth of the Spirit Tree opened, red and midnight marbled. Its throat was deep and white with the bones of a million beasts.

The pod released them. Caracol clung to the beautiful black fur.

Hunter and prey. The safety of dark and the smell of my little one near me.

The Love Theatre

Mason Yeater

Projectionist | A Missing Notebook

Being Other People

I sit in my booth as the reel purrs. This one is about two high school seniors who try to cram in as many dates as they can before they leave for separate universities. Mini golf, an aquarium, a palm reader, a carnival. Every date they pretend they're different people. It's sweet. They don't want to admit how much they care about each other so one girl pretends she's into hockey and the other wears a Lolita dress.

It's important to have a sense of humor when you're courting someone. I used to laugh and laugh before my ex left me.

They get to the scene where the girls meet up and realize they're both dressed like the other girl. They didn't plan it so now you know they're really in love. The booth is soundproofed but I hear the audience hum. They like it. I smell the oils on their popcorn. I'm starving for a kiss. This is when I notice my notebook is gone.

We Three Kings

It's not gone exactly. There's another notebook on the table of my booth. Same black cover, the elastic band, the sticker on the lower right-hand corner of a cartoon heart. But all of the pages are blank.

I've already laced up the film for the other screen and I have five other prints to inspect and splice this week, so I have to stay focused. Our theatre, whose sole speciality is romance, has two screens: one for the feature and the other for events and seasonal films. My booth looks over both of them. I really could watch people fall in love forever. But I've been feeling strange all day, like if someone asked me my name it would take a second to remember it.

It's December so I just started showing this film. Three princes from rival nations in Europe are summoned to a small, neutral country that borders all three. It's a tree-decorating competition. The premise is silly, and not just because the countries are fictional and the kings are princes not kings, but that's why I love it. At first they all hate each other because they have different traditions: one only dresses in white, the other's banned sweets, and the third carries a lute wherever he goes. But the Christmas spirit overpowers them in the end and they learn to appreciate their differences to decorate the most beautiful tree in the competition's history. They don't technically kiss, but the last scene shows them sharing a king-sized bed, so this is the fourth year I've played it.

Normally my stomach tickles with blood when I watch them slowly change their minds but today I don't feel much of anything. I keep thinking of my ex who came by this morning to pick up the last of his stuff. A beat-up coffee grinder and a t-shirt from one of our first dates. The one at the planetarium. I was surprised he even wanted it. He was the one who ended things. But I always like to see him, so I let him in.

Orphan Trail

The next day is even worse. I barely have the energy to lift the new reels that come in. Their silver shipping containers feel like anchors. This film is older so I take my time checking for damage. But it's clean, no tears, very little dust. After it's spliced I let it play. Sometimes an audience of one is the most romantic way to watch a movie. I spend almost all my time alone, so I would know. It's the wanting. The sort of energy that could keep me alive for a second lifetime.

It's in color but the picture is mostly shades of tan, sometimes a pale blue sky and the film grain. A widow's son goes missing on the frontier. She's hopeless so she drinks herself into a stupor at the saloon. But a gunslinger walks in, says two lines that are barely audible, and carries her back to his campsite on his horse.

He knows where the kid is. She tells him she would do anything for her child. He tells her he would do anything for her. She's mostly sober and half smiling. They make love under the stars. It's the wordless honesty.

I want to retch. Nausea invades like rotten bubbles popping in my torso. Where is my journal?

Mr. & Mrs. Sleeper

He switched them. I let him in, offered to make him tea. He said yes, but he left as soon as he found that shirt in the bedroom. That's where I keep my notebook. I should have known. Love means trust. He could be insecure. Yes, I wrote about us. Even the time he refused to speak to me. When he did speak and told me I made him smaller when I touched him. That I was clingy. But I smelled him and there was fear wafting from his skin. What does he think I would do with that story?

There's no use. It's just paper anyway. I have another film to process.

It's a spy movie. They're not married but might as well be. They work flawlessly on their own, never get lonely, never need anything. He photographs secret military technologies overseas. She lives undercover, memorizing documents in a foreign agency, transcribing them back in her apartment at night. That they will save their nation from the evils of anticapitalist regimes is secondary to the plot. Their meetings are always brief, vodka and shadows, but filled with a quiet understanding that this is all they have and it is enough. The independence that grounds their relationship. The backbone that grows from their self-sufficiency. It's farcical. How can they have a deep love when they work thousands of miles apart? What good is passion when it only lasts a night? I would take him, bowtie and acetate fingers, take his hands into mine, teeth to my teeth, feel the slopes of his skin as my own. With my kiss. With my kiss I would take her too, perfume and tumbler, and never let them go.

A Lifetime to Centauri

The theatre is full. I peek through the porthole for a while to watch them chatter. I like to imagine the conversations before their minds empty, all filling with the same thoughts.

This one is set on a generation ship. Earth is dead. The ship is so large they don't meet until their early twenties. That's when they find out they'll be the last generation to die on the ship, before it reaches the planet that's meant to be the future of humanity. Their kids, if they have any, might stain their feet with real soil in their sixties. As months pass, they shift from denial and madness to pure acceptance. They learn to savor the tiny pleasures of their day-to-day, the walks across the starry bay, poems written in the old world surviving in fading hardcover.

All life is transient. So why should they cheat themselves of that beauty? I watch the audience wipe their cheeks as the couple embraces their end. I watch them pull tissues from their purses, clasp their partners' hands as the couple resolves to lay their first eyes on that distant star, Centauri, to finally accept its unreachable salvation. I wonder if they understand that another human being offers nothing under mortality's vaulted face. Its features rise beyond their sight as it takes them into its black jaws, and memories will vanish like mist in the morning sun.

Conjure Me

My journal. Without those pages all of this is meaningless. I try to remember why I'm here. I run the film through my fingers. Slippery, slippery moments. In that notebook I wrote everything I learned of love. What were those things? My cells reject the memories. That is why I kept them in paper. My ex is afraid of me. That is why he took it. He would stare at me from across the apartment, watched me when I boiled water, when I slept. When he thought I wouldn't notice. If he wants evidence, he won't have it. There is nothing but sincerity in those pages. I want to love. I wanted love. Before he stole my only means. To know humor and compromise and honesty and trust. These are just words now.

I play this film for myself. Sit in the empty theatre. It's so hot in my seats, and strange to hear these people speaking from the screen. A woman is lonely, unbearably. She finds an old book at an estate sale. Takes it back to her house, sets up in her den, lighting candles in a semicircle. As she reads aloud the dead language, a man emerges from the shadows. They talk. He's handsome, of course, but a specter, so they can never touch. This kills her. Voiceover reveals he's the one telling the story. Either this means the ending is very happy or very sad. The way he reflects, his even melancholy. I try to imagine what I would think of this with my journal still in my hands. Would she kill herself to become like him? So they could entangle phantom limbs? Or would it go wrong? Would she simply die? Would her ghost shiver, shrink, her soul sucked elsewhere?

I don't know because I lose interest. I remember who I used to be before I learned to journal. I walk into the street. It's after midnight and I'm hungry.

The Tides of Mallorca

His condo is vacant. He moved without telling me. I wonder when the police will come with questions. I'll see him for what he's taken. He never tried to understand me. Once he found a flaw it bred like germs, and in his eyes it became my entire image. I wanted human love. That was all. It took months to gather those notes and now. Now why would I ever want to collect them again? Those pieces would make for a crooked puzzle. But there's no rush to find him. That will be easy. He reeks and I can smell him now from my booth.

This film was a critical darling in its time, with no shortage of skin. The audience knows this. They're packed in, every seat in my hot, hot room. The rumbling of their voices. The room goes black.

In the 30s two men flee from the Spanish mainland to Mallorca. They're in love. Of course they are. This is my theatre. The authorities are tracking them. One is a sex worker. He was entrapped but escaped, using the officer's own cuffs against him. Now they're both on the run, living every day in paranoid agony and selfless passion. I know the ending. Everyone does. They lie together in a shabby, dawn-lit bed and wonder if they'll last another night.

He never saw who I am, but does he wonder this too, in his new bed? He caught slivers through the curtain I fastened around his life. What he thinks he knows of me is an abyss seen only from the bottom. He won't look up until I let him. Tonight he will open his eyes and search madly for the pinprick of light overhead, all those many miles down.

When I put the projector to sleep and wipe my lips of my kiss, I think of what could have been. If he had let me, I would love him still. A better love for him than this. This is a promise as I take a last look at the white-limned shadows of the theatre, admiring all their necks unbuttoned. I lock the entrance and follow his stench down the sidewalk of the city.

The Vault

Jonathan M. Wolf

Laser Operator | Unreadable Handwriting

Brennan Miles' hands dig deep into the guts of a specialized precision laser, searching the guts for the connective wires he needs. He calls the laser *Demetrius*, and in just a few moments Brennan will use Demetrius to cut through the jet-black walls of the monolithic chamber in the center of the room, thoughtfully dubbed "the vault."

That is, he will if he can get the damn thing working. He's been piecing the thing together for a week now, although it should have been finished two days ago. He doesn't tell the others it's his fault for putting the thing together wrong. *Three times.*

"I heard Brennan's got a *date*," says Karl. He's in charge of translating the ancient writing that's been hand-carved into the walls maybe two hundred centuries ago, and he's got his lackey, Jim, "the new guy," scanning every inch of the place with a digital camera to feed into their computer software.

"With *who?*" Kayla butts in. She's sitting on the stone floor, back against a wall, studying something on a tablet. The digital sort, not an ancient one. Some pottery, or something, rests next to her. Excepting Brennan, they've all been working at the Dig for months, even Jim.

"With whatever's in that vault," Brennan grins. He finds the bundle of wires he's been after and pulls them free, then shoves them back into the guts of the laser. In the *right* spot this time.

"Yeah, if you ever get that laser working," shoots Karl.

Lemont pokes his head from behind the vault, an ominous black monolith at the center of the dusty room. "Let the man work," he calls out, "I wanna see him blast a giant hole in this vault with the most powerful laser in the world."

"Not a vault," insists Kayla without even looking up.

"It's about precision, not power," says Brennan, "Something every woman has tried to explain to Karl, but he just won't learn."

"Oooh," says Jim, but he tapers off when Karl shoots him a dirty look.

"Not a vault," says Kayla. "It's a cage."

"Won't know for sure 'til Demetrius here gently unlocks the door," says Brennan. He slams the casing down with a satisfactory chunk and dusts off his hands, then picks up a rag to wipe the sweat off his face. He coughs, not used to the combination of chill air and dust that pervades every chamber in the dig. "Which is about to happen, because she's online."

"Hell yeah," says Karl.

At that moment, Suzanne—Dr. Guilding, Ph.D—flies into the room. Her large curly red hair bounces fluffily behind her, trying to keep up, and she looks slightly frazzled as always. "Are we in the vault yet?" she asks, staring at Brennan.

"Just gotta calibrate."

Brennan holds up what looks like a flashlight, shining its intense beam at the vault door. He holds it there for a few moments, then twists a few dials and flicks a few switches on the laser's control panel. Suzanne steps back, clutches her clipboard to her chest, studies Brennan carefully as he works.

"You're all about to be impressed," Brennan says. His hand hovers above a glowing blue switch. Everyone holds their breath, their eyes locked on the hovering finger. It's about to happen; a vault closed for untold centuries will have been opened, its mysteries unveiled. Hearts are beating fast.

"Wait!" shouts Karl. Everyone's heart nearly stops. "Can't you read the sign?"

Karl points to the writing above the vault door urgently, as if it were flashing red and blaring alarms. Brennan raises an eyebrow.

"Oh yeah, me neither," laughs Karl. He taps a few buttons on his laptop and reads the screen. "My translator A.I. thinks it might say 'Cursed be he who crosses this portal.' Well... ten percent confidence on that one. Could be 'Vault of the King's Riches.' Eight percent. Ooh, I like this one. 'A blind man enters the silence.'"

Brennan smirks, shakes his head, and presses the blue button with no further hesitation. "I apologize if we all get zapped into another dimension. Or someone gets superpowers."

Servo motors hum. The emitter tilts and turns into position.

Silence.

"Ahem," says Jim, "I sort of expected, ah..."

"It's working. Precision," Brennan says, "It's removing one layer of atoms at a time. Give it a minute. Hey, where did Suzanne go?"

"Doctor Guilding?" Karl glances around. The rest of them shrug; no one remembers seeing her leave, but she is head of the whole Dig. Likely someone called her away on some new trouble— or some new discovery.

The laser continues its silent, invisible work, but as the seconds tick by, one atom at a time, there becomes a noticeable, although indescribable change. The laser apparatus beeps, and a light flashes.

"It's done," says Brennan. He walks to the door and puts his fingers at the crevice. "Help me out here."

Lemont jumps in next to Brennan and jams his own fingers in. Between them, they manage to pry the door out of its socket. It hardly creaks on its hinges as they swing it open, and they carefully lay the door to rest, fully open. Brennan sticks his head in.

"Well, what's in there?" asks Kayla. The tone in her voice betrayed an urgency that she'd hid up to that moment. "Is it the secret to reality itself? The king's treasure? A pile of rusty manacles?"

"Nothing," says Brennan. He can't hide the disappointment in his voice, but he also can't lie. The vault is empty, filled with nothing but old air and shadows. No treasure, no ancient remains of prisoners. Hardly any dust. Just four grey walls. And shadows.

"Ah, shit," says Karl.

Something wavers in a dark corner of Brennan's mind, the he can't shake. Something about... the shadows. A queasy feeling arises in his stomach. "I've gotta get some fresh air," he says. He takes a step, but stops and looks back. He can't shake a feeling, an indescribable feeling. Like something *was* in the vault and had now been freed, but someone would have seen it. They *all* would have seen it. But it is there, a gut feeling. Brennan breaths and walks out, muttering: "I'll see you all tonight at the Eagle."

"No you won't," Karl says, too late. "Hot date, remember?"

***

Something seems wrong.

It's like the world has gotten quieter.

Hours later. Brennan has a date in 20 minutes—he hasn't forgotten. He's had time to take a shower, clear his mind. Get over the disappointment of failure.

It's not working. His stomach feels... off. No, his *brain*. He's holding his phone in his hand, and he tries to call Karl, yet again. The call connects, but there's no answer. Just a soft clicking sound, or maybe nothing.

"Hello? Karl, are you messing with me?" asks Brennan. No answer. He hits *end call* and drops the phone. He has to go, so he gave up bothering to call any of the others. Jim, Suzanne, Kayla. Lemont. For the third time.

A bus takes him to Andre's, the restaurant he'd planned to meet his date. The bus isn't crowded, but the people on it stare at him, and not pleasantly. At least it feels that way. Brennan shudders, looks out the window, and ditches the bus three blocks early to walk the rest of the way.

When at last he catches sight of his date, his stomach starts to feel a little better. Angelina is beautiful; wearing a simple black dress that drapes loosely over her body, her shoulder-length, shiny, wavy, black hair hangs perfectly in place. A silver necklace adorns her neck. She barely knows him, and he barely knows her, which is ideal. They were set up by mutual friends, and had only texted a few times before tonight. There was plenty to talk about besides work, and failed projects.

Andre's is usually bustling with crowds, but tonight half the seats are empty. It's a dimly lit dining room, filled with warmth and ambiance, and a little quietness didn't hurt at all. Brennan did make a reservation earlier, but the maître d' refused to sit them immediately, insisting they would be seated the moment their table was ready. Brennan insisted right back that clearly, there were tables available.

Again with the weird looks, even from Angelina. Brennan tries to shake off the impatience, and they stand in awkward silence, until at last they are brought to a seat.

"I'm sorry," says Brennan, "I've been on the edge. Rough day at work. Maybe we can start over?"

Angelina smiles cautiously, and for some time things do go better. Brennan does well at first meetings; He speaks comfortably, asks questions, she responds warmly, and he forgets the shadows in the corner of his brain.

Until.

About halfway through dinner, Brennan locks his gaze on an older couple dining in a booth not ten feet away. Only, the booth is empty, completely empty, but Brennan is certain an elderly couple had been dining there moments earlier.

In fact, as he looks around, Brennan realizes the restaurant is emptier than before. The light seems dull and grey now, not warm and inviting.

"Does it seem… empty, in here, to you?"

Angelina looks at him, just like everyone's been looking at him all day. Like he's insane. Like he's just shoved an old lady into the street just to get to a crosswalk before the light turns red.

"Are you… feeling all right?" Angelina asks.

Brennan shakes his head. The shadow in his mind has come back. He rests his chin on his hands, stares across the room. It's not just quiet… it's *empty*. As if everyone at the same moment abandoned their plate and rushed out, like the fire alarm had been pulled. Only, no sound of an alarm, no rush that Brennan had noticed.

"What the hell is…" Brennan starts to say, but he jumps back into his chair. Angelina is gone.

Brennan stands up so quickly his chair falls over. His heart pounds. He turns. He runs.

A city doesn't exist without its bustling life force, but the streets are nearly empty. One or two cars pass on the entire journey to The Eagle, at least eight blocks. Brennan arrives there, out of breath. It isn't empty, but the crowds are much smaller than usual. At least that makes it easy to find his coworkers, but it's only Karl, Suzanne, and what looks like a few other members of the larger team that Brennan doesn't know. He starts towards them, then freezes.

They look blurry. Out of focus. They look like… shadows. Brennan's heartbeat accelerates to five thousand beats per second. They just sit there, talking to each other. They don't notice what's happening to them. They don't realize they're fading, and it's too late. He stumbles backwards until his back touches the wall, and he sinks down.

They are gone. They're all gone.

Brennan fights back tears. He pulls out his phone and stares at it. Who to call? Angelina? She's gone. Jim? Gone. Karl? Suzanne?

There are no cars on the streets. No bodies or voices in the bar. The streetlights are dim.

The world fills with shadows.

***

Karl, Jim, Suzanne, Kayla, and Lemont sip their drinks, passing quiet glances between each other. A dozen or so others from the Dig sit or stand nearby, most cheerful and excited for the next day's dig. The rest of the crowded bar bustles noisily, but the five of them can't help but keep an eye on Brennan who sits with his back to the wall, on the floor, in the corner.

"What's up with Brennan?" asks Kayla.

"Yeah," says Lemont, "He called me like three times and shouted hello, but he acted like he couldn't hear me."

Karl takes one long draught from his glass, and shrugs. "Must have been a bad date."

The Translation of Nina

Aggie Novak

Linguist | Shadows

Dead languages cast the longest shadows. That's what Alice's girlfriend—late girlfriend—Nina always said. The roots of their words reach through time and spread through cultures. Alice disagreed. Dead *linguists* cast the longest shadows. That's what Nina's death was: a vast spectre haunting Alice's life, darkening everything.

Alice slumped back in the taxi and stared out the grimy window, sucking at her lower lip to keep from crying. This wasn't how her long-awaited trip to St Petersburg was supposed to go. The city centre, at least, was as beautiful as Nina promised. As they left the airport behind, endless soviet apartment blocks gave way to the sort of European architecture Alice would expect of Venice or Paris. The endless grey interrupted with pale blues and yellows, and ornamented facades. All those places Nina planned to show her.

Alice looked away and unlocked her phone. In a painful habit she'd developed over the last three days, she opened her last message from Nina.

I'm not sure you should come anymore.

Alice's frantic questions had all been met with silence. Until she got a message from an unknown number.

You are Alice? Good friend of Nina?

Sorry, who is this?

Polina. Nina's flatmate. *You are Alice?*

Yes, what's up?

Nina died.

Not sure what else there was to do, Alice had caught her flight anyway. She'd never met Nina's family. All she knew was that they didn't approve of Alice, Nina's linguistic career, or her current stay in Russia. When Alice messaged her condolences, all they said in reply was that they'd be going to St Petersburg in a week to repatriate Nina's body and collect her belongings. That if Alice could afford the airfare—unlikely—she'd be welcome in Philadelphia for the funeral.

That gave her four days to figure out what happened. Four days to figure out why her girlfriend killed herself, just when everything had been going so well.

This is it, Al. My big break. I'll be able to get a stable position. We can finally live together properly.

Al, it's beautiful here. You'll love it. I've found the perfect spot to celebrate our anniversary.

I can't wait for your visit, Al. I miss you.

Some of her messages had been a little strange. Late-night linguistic musings and mentions of nightmares.

It's like this translation is possessing me, Al. Like the true meaning is just there, waiting to be let out. I just have to get it right.

I'm so close. It's amazing, Al, bringing something forgotten to life.

Did I ever wake up screaming when we lived together? Polina said she thought I was being murdered.

But Alice thought it was just run-of-the-mill stress, maybe a bit too much work and too little sleep. Nothing to really worry about.

Nina's apartment building stretched the length of the block, punctuated by a series of identical metal doors streaked with damp.

The taxi deposited her outside the correct one, leaving Alice and her single suitcase standing on the slushy curb. Above, yellow hazard tape fluttered from the top floor balcony. Alice looked away and pushed the intercom button for apartment twenty-five.

"Allo?"

"It's Alice."

There was no reply, but the door clicked open. A grand staircase with wide stone steps spiralled up to the next floor. But it was also filthy. Old wrappers and muddy boot-prints littered the floor, the green-painted walls flaked, and exposed wires ran above doors. She trudged up the uneven steps to the fifth floor, where a woman—Polina—waited in a doorway.

"Welcome," she said, unsmiling.

"Hi, um, thanks." Alice quickly followed her in.

Polina pointed to a pile of runners and winter boots. "Put shoes here." She looked Alice up and down. "You speak Russian?"

"Um, no. Sorry."

Polina shrugged. "You are hungry?"

"Um, no, no thank you. I'd like to rest."

Another shrug. "You can take food from fridge. No problem."

"Thanks. Thank you so much for letting me stay." Alice tried a smile, but it felt feeble and false.

Polina took her bag and wheeled it down the hall to a door. "This is Nina's room. Everything is there."

Polina watched Alice stand outside the bedroom door. It had a high, old-fashioned doorknob, tarnished by a thick layer of green. Trapped between Polina, who clearly expected her to go in, and whatever was left of Nina, Alice chose the latter.

The room was high-ceilinged and huge—and almost completely empty. A lone armoire rested against one wall, opposite the double bed. Its floral coverlet clashed hideously with the dark blue and gold royal wallpaper. The only other furniture in the room was a small desk and chair right in front of the glass door leading to the balcony. Luckily, the sheer white curtains were drawn tight, but they did little to block out the gloomy light. It was pristine, the floor clear and the bedspread smooth.

Nina had always been so messy, back home.

Maybe Polina cleaned up. Alice could ask her, but the thought of standing for a moment longer was too much. She flopped onto the bed and buried her face in the soft, lumpy pillows. The faint smell of rose shampoo might be the most she had left of Nina. Alice pulled back the covers, ready to cocoon herself in the scent, and screamed.

A crow, wings spread, and neck bent, gazed up at her with dead eyes.

She shrieked again and scrambled from the bed.

The door crashed open and Polina flicked on the light. "What is it?"

Alice pointed, shaking. "That. Why is there a dead bird in the bed?

Polina scrunched up her nose. "I don't know, I'm sorry." She shrugged and gestured to the wall behind the bed. "Nina was a bit...odd, yes?"

She hadn't noticed in the dim light, the dark film blending into the wallpaper, but there were six chest X-rays stuck—no, *nailed*—in a row. Alice leaned closer and squinted at them. There were no names, but each was labelled with a date, one month apart. The latest was from last week. White shadows speckled the lungs in each scan, getting progressively worse.

Do you ever feel like you can't breathe?

Alice thought Nina had been referring to her panic attacks, but this...

She cleared her throat and forced out a reply. "I suppose she was."

Alice wouldn't have said she was put-a-dead-bird-in-her-bed odd, but she wouldn't have guessed she was jump-to-her-death depressed either. "What should I do with the bird?"

"Throw it out the window."

Blood crusted its beak and stained the pastel green sheet beneath it.

When Alice didn't move, Polina grabbed it by the tip of one wing, parted the curtains and chucked it out.

Alice couldn't shake the image of Nina plummeting to the street just like the crow.

"Thanks," she croaked. "I'm going to rest for a bit."

As soon as Polina shut the door, she ripped the X-rays from the wall and tossed them to the bed. Then she stripped the sheets and pushed them onto the floor. She didn't lie back down. Instead, she opened the armoire. A tangle of crumpled clothes greeted her. Coats, shoes, bras and shirts shoved in with no thought given to organisation. Alice smiled and pulled out Nina's favourite oversized jumper. She slipped it on and snuggled into it.

Able to pretend, just for a bit, that Nina was with her, soft against her skin, Alice made herself go to the desk. Nina's research, the translation and analysis of a recently discovered text—which experts thought was the first solid evidence of the Proto-Slavic language—brought her to Russia to begin with. And she had been *enthralled* by it. That was the only word Alice could think of for the mixture of obsession and enthusiasm that had possessed Nina.

Her messages had been full of—to Alice, incomprehensible—gushing about velar palatalisation and Havlík's law. About the intellectual magic of deciphering the mother of all Slavic languages. The text would be the foundation of the rest of Nina's academic career. MIT would be scrambling to hire her.

Alice, desperate to find something in her girlfriend's work she understood, had asked what the text was about.

It appears to be a folk story.

That was firmer territory. *Wow. I thought you were going to say a biography of some man. Are there house spirits? Or forest nymphs?*

We think it could be about a Mora or Nocnitsa. A demon of nightmares.

An unsteady stack of books, sheets of paper, and a dented MacBook covered the desk. The books meant nothing to Alice—they had titles in Cyrillic she couldn't parse. She gathered the loose papers instead, some of them tucked between the pages of the books, all covered in Nina's looping scrawl.

Some sources suggest birds of prey as a ward. Worth a try?

A ward? Alice flicked through the notes.

Every night, the pressure on my chest grows heavier. The doctors say nothing is wrong, but I see the shadows on the scans.

Accounts of night-terrors and straining lungs were interspersed with notes in Russian and lists of unfamiliar words written out in IPA.

I think my translation did something. I think I unlocked more than just the meaning of forgotten words.

But how were dead crows and Old East Slavic linguistics linked? Clearly Nina had thought they were.

Alice pushed the papers aside and flipped open the laptop. The profile picture was of her and Nina grinning outside a cute cafe in Tallinn, their cheeks pink with cold and wind. Alice typed in her birthday and breathed a sigh of relief when it worked.

There were three windows and about a hundred tabs open—a bunch on folklore about *Mora*, endless linguistics articles, medical FAQs on lung cancer, 'Could you be possessed?' quizzes. Alice minimised them and opened Word instead. Only one untitled document was open.

I wanted to send this as an email, but it wouldn't let me. Maybe someone will see it. I'm going to burn it. The original and translation both. I stole the text, but the consequences won't matter. I won't let it spread. I love you, Alice.

A suicide note. Alice ducked under the desk and grabbed the small bin, sure she was about to be sick.

Scorch marks blackened the sides and curls of ash dusted the bottom. And laying on top was an unmarred document, typed in clear Calibri.

Alice read.

Of the Deepest Lore and True History Concerning the Mother of Shadows and Fears of the Slavs.

Nina's translation. She had died for the words on this paper. They'd both read folktales before—the sweet Disney kind and the babies-in-pies kind—but something about this one had both captivated and terrified Nina. She had to know. Settling on the floor, back pressed against the end of the bed, Alice began to read.

***

A dark shadow loomed in the corner of the ceiling, then rushed down with a flash of red eyes. Alice tried to shout for help, but a heavy pressure settled around her chest. It was hard to breathe. She couldn't make a sound.

She jerked awake, gasping for breath, chest tight and heart thudding in her mouth. She rolled her neck, stiff from the awkward position. Better than sleeping where the crow had been.

In one hand, she still gripped Nina's translation. It would be wrong for her life's work to be discarded, tossed out in the trash. Nina had accomplished something extraordinary, and she deserved to be remembered for it.

She went to the laptop, opened Gmail, and found the email address of Nina's supervisor.

Dear Professor Zharkov,

This is Nina's dear friend, Alice. I found this translation in Nina's notes, and I'm sure she would have wanted you to have them. I would be happy to meet and return the rest of her research.

Best, Alice.

That done, she closed the laptop and made her way through the apartment to the kitchen, taking in the drab surroundings.

"Polina, are you awake?" she called. "I'm hungry now."

The Dog in the Glass Jar

Sean Fallon

Butterfly Collector | Lost Dog

Content Warning: Animal death

Tell me your story, and I'll tell you mine.

Tell me about the dog. The dog in the glass jar.

Tell me how you found it. How it looked, smelt, sounded. It was dead, obviously, but the smell of formaldehyde would be cloying. It smells like pickles, formaldehyde, which is distressing when you think of dead loved ones who were embalmed but really they just pickled. Like gherkins.

The dog was a mongrel retriever mix thing. Through the murk of the preservation chemical you could guess it had been brown and black in life. But the liquid had turned foggy and greenish with age.

It was, weirdly, in a wooden cabinet that stood in the corridor of a school. Housed near the science labs so that made it slightly less weird, but in a place where children spent their day, it felt ghoulish and somehow threatening to have this dog in its jar just there for all to see.

You had gone to that school to meet the butterfly collector. He was the science teacher and a man of incalculable age as he had silver hair but an unlined face. He walked with a cane but spoke with clarity and surety that attested to a clear, young mind. His students loved and reviled him in equal measure because he was a teacher, after all, and tossed on the waves of the capricious opinions of teenagers.

The butterfly collection he had was legendary among lepidopterist groups, one of which you frequented.

Lovely word, *lepidopterist*. One of those wonderful crossword answer words like philatelist, campanologist, or toxofolist. Technical terms that felt more poetic than simply saying stamp collector, bell ringer, and archer.

What you didn't know about the butterfly collector, and what you would soon learn, was that he'd grown weary of butterfly collecting. He had collected as many as he could and had amassed a collection of the rarest breeds like the Miami Blue, the Zebra Longwing, and the Blue Morpho.

They all sat in wooden cases, pinned to boards behind glass. As a butterfly collector yourself, you knew the process. You got a killing jar and a butterfly. Put the butterfly in the jar with some ethyl acetate and it would be poisoned quickly and painlessly. Fun fact, grasshoppers in the jar kicked off their hind legs while dying.

Once you had killed your butterfly you could spread it out and pin it to your styrofoam board with a size 2 pin right through the middle of its thorax. Place that in a case and display your beautiful handiwork.

If you hear the wings flapping at night while you're trying to sleep, just try to ignore it.

It's gone out of fashion, insect collecting. I blame the killing jar. If they found a sweeter name maybe it wouldn't rub people the wrong way. So perhaps we'll call it the Sleeping Glass.

When you get directions to the *lepidopterist* (though you call him a butterfly collector so as to not sound pretentious), you'll be told to take a left at the dog in the glass jar.

When you see the dog, you won't think Sleeping Glass. You'll think dead dog. And even though you don't know that your fate and the dog's fate will eventually rhyme like a poem in a child's book, at that moment the emotion you feel towards the dog in the glass jar is empathy.

You wonder, was this a scientist's dog? Did the dog die and the scientist chose to preserve it forever in a vain stab at immortality? Was it a lost dog that an owner searched and searched for but never found and now, when they lie in bed at night, they beat themselves up for not locking a gate or not handing out enough MISSING DOG flyers?

Was it even a real dog?

While you waited for the butterfly collector to see you, you stared into the eyes of the dog and see that yes, the hot fire of life once filled this dog to the brim. It had been one of the grand creatures of the Earth and now it floats in a jar filled with chemicals the color of overripe avocado.

The butterfly collector took you into his classroom and then the office that adjoined it.

The first thing you noticed was the lack of butterflies. On the bus ride over, you imagined butterfly cases filling every surface. Colors would explode from every surface, mixing in a delightful feast that would satiate your eyes until they were fit to burst in your skull.

Alas, it was not that at all. It was bare walls and an orderly desk. It looked like a showroom in an incredibly boring IKEA. The dead dog in the jar had more life.

There was a smell though. Nail polish remover. That strong chemical smell that reminds you of your grandmother taking off her makeup or a butterfly flapping its last.

The butterfly collector greeted you, offered you tea or coffee. You chose one but that's unimportant as he'd drugged both.

Before it kicked in — the Flunitrazepam in the tea, that is — the butterfly collector explained that his collection was currently kept in storage. He found being surrounded by tiny deaths had begun to weigh upon him. The flapping of a dying butterfly is such a small sound and yet, like a ringing in his ears, he found it lingered. And then when the sound vanished he became despondent so would seek out more butterflies. Over and over until the sound simply stopped.

The butterfly collector read somewhere that when a loud noise causes a ringing in your ear, that noise is the death cry of that frequency. Once it is gone, it's gone. The butterfly collector thought he had done something similar with the sound of the wings. The part of his ear and his brain that heard it was gone.

Your eyes drooped, your mouth tried to form words like *what* and *help*. It was no use as the wires that connected your brain to your mouth were clogged with a drug that strangled all communication like an army that shoots messengers on the battlefield.

The butterfly collector told you about the dog. It was a lost dog, he said, proving you right though you took no joy in that as you struggled to rise from your chair before falling back into it. The dog had a collar, a name, a phone number to call. The butterfly collector burnt that collar afterwards. He needed no souvenirs save the glass jar and the floating dog.

The amount of ethyl acetate needed to kill a butterfly was measured in droplets. The amount to kill a dog? Considerably more but, like the butterfly, it was a quick, seemingly painless process.

Obtaining a big enough glass jar was a chore that involved all manner of internet sleuthing until the butterfly collector found a company that made glass jars, bottles, artworks, etc. to order for exorbitant fees but nothing that broke the bank, and the formaldehyde came from a medical wholesaler.

The hardest part had been convincing the principal that the dog in the glass jar had a place in the school corridor, but since the principal was more worried about school shootings and teen pregnancies, he didn't put up too much of a fight.

You, on the other hand, can't be displayed in a school cabinet, as you probably could understand. You raised a hand and gurgled something, but it was a moot point now.

The butterfly collector sat on his desk and waited until you slumped further and further into the chair. There would be no glass jar for you. Ordering one for a person would cost too much and be hard to store. For you, the butterfly collector had set aside a space on his basement wall. He would spread your wings, so to speak, and then drive a metal spike - made in the shop class of the school you were passing out in - straight through your thorax or as its known in humans, your thoracic cavity.

After that, who knows? Maybe the butterfly collector would find a bigger animal to kill or maybe he would just stop. Maybe the flapping noise would return, maybe it wouldn't.

The problem the butterfly collector faced in the end though was not how to move you without being seen, or how much ethyl acetate would be needed to kill you. No, the problem was that you had exaggerated your symptoms. You had become drowsy and could feel yourself slipping so you pretended to slip faster than you actually were. And then, when the butterfly collector was telling you all about your upcoming fate, you lunged from your chair, grabbed the letter opener that lay on his desk, the one with the gold butterfly inlay on the handle, and you stabbed it not into his thoracic cavity, but into his throat.

As you slipped to the floor, you brought the letter opener with you, opening the wound and splashing those plain, lifeless walls with the heart-hot blood of the butterfly collector.

After that, you did pass out and when you came to you were in the hospital where you stayed under observation for two days before being released. And then you came back to the school for a final piece of business: retrieving the dog in the glass jar. This way it could be laid to rest with respect rather than being something for teenagers to gawk at.

While you decided where to bury the dog, you put the glass jar on a desk in your bedroom and you slept in its shadow. And every night you would dream that you and it exchanged stories about lost dogs and butterfly collectors. Murderers and the murdered. Killing jars and sleeping glasses.

And somewhere in the house, a butterfly flapped its wings.

Into the Gray

Nicole Lovell

Magnet Fisherman | A Conspiracy

I'm slipping into the gray again; I feel it seeping in early this year like fog at the peripherals of my mind.

Outside, Summer and Fall are mingling at a crossroads. Afternoon sun still bathes the earth in warmth, yet evenings winds whisper prophecy of a bitter cold looming just over the Autumn horizon. Trees explode with color; leaves transforming to crimsons, oranges, yellows, and timber browns - nature's palette. The shrill orchestral buzz of cicadas has begun a slow descent into silence. Fall has always been my favorite season because of this metamorphosis - a stunning transitional dance which eases us into a pallid winter.

Inside, I will not be afforded such a graceful descent into the dreary this year. The four walls of my bedroom are once again becoming my closest companions. It's 2 am and sleep eludes me as it has for the last three nights. So I scroll, and scroll. Anything to quiet my thoughts, to ease the pain of introspection.

Twelve months, officially, as of midnight. One full year since I left my little hometown, my sister, my life. My abuser. One year since Quincy police took his side after he trashed our home. "There's nothing we can do, it's his property too" they shrugged. "Just give each other some space, imagine the makeup sex heh" the senior one quipped, as bile rose into my esophagus. They stood casually by their cruisers, chatting with him. I tip-toed around shattered glass, hiding important documents. That night I cleaned while he slept in his recliner, whiskey still in hand. In the morning I apologized for making him angry, and sent him to work with lunch.

Two hours later I was at my sister, Ivy's, kitchen table, sobbing in front of her and her husband Jack. "I've been ready for this, little Bug" Ivy whispered, wiping tears from my cheeks. With the gentle touch of an older sister, she cradled my locket in her left hand while gripping her own in her right. Our mother gave them to us when we were 14 and 16 - just weeks before her death. The lockets are unique, custom made with a heart shaped emerald in the center. Ivy and I have worn them devotedly since. "I'm here for you. I'm going to help you start over, Sam". And she did.

***

He left town silently three months after I did, but I can never return. 218 miles away, I'm thriving at my job, working remotely - something my agoraphobia agrees with. I have both a psychiatrist and therapist I trust. Abuse and trauma were familiar foes long before him; only now do I fully see the pattern. The healing process has been trying and although I know I'm safer now, some days take more than I have to give. Most winters, regular depression shifts into something bleaker, but this year feels different. I am inundated with internal chatter. So I scroll.

Dance trend, *swipe*. Palestinian Chicken recipe, *save*. Goats cuddling cats, *heart*. Lesbian thirst trap…*pause, swipe*.

My eyes grow heavy but my anxious mind fights sleep. Wait, what was that? I swipe back, neurons firing off a message of recognition. Whoa, is that Craven Bridge? It is! I played muddy soccer by this creek all the time in Elementary school. The video is in first person perspective, camera must be strapped to their head. Black gloves grip a worn rope hanging over the bridge, hand over hand dragging something in from the water. Wordlessly they pull up a rusted wrench and nails clinging to a large magnet. Oh, I've heard of magnet fishing. The video ends unceremoniously. I tap their name, MagMan, and investigate. Huh, the account must be new - 30 followers and three other videos. I vaguely recognize locations in two of them. What are the odds? I tap follow.

It's 3 AM now. I'll scroll until I fall asleep. Note to self: talk to Dr. Reed about adjusting meds for the season.

***

PING!

A notification alerts me that MagMan has uploaded. It'll be his sixth new video in the two weeks since I followed. All of them equally boring. He works in a cluster of towns around Quincy, though, and watching connects me to home. Yesterday I left a comment of support, hoping he doesn't quit. I miss Quincy.

I open today's video expecting the usual, and at first that's what I get. First person POV, gloved hands, rope, silence. This time, though, as the magnet breaks the surface, water comes cascading down the sides of a small black safe. A flicker of anticipation unfurls from my stomach up into my chest. I'm glued to the screen. He breaks open the safe, and water pours out revealing various pieces of jewelry. The video ends abruptly. "Oh come on!"

***

It's 10 am and I'm just now opening my bedroom curtains to let in a sliver of light. I called in sick this morning, leaving out the fact that I'm plagued by insomnia - not a virus. Rewatching MagMan's videos has become part of my nightly routine. I like to think it connects me to home and saves me from late night rumination. A voice in my head says it's actually the reason for my sleepless nights; I ignore it.

PING!

In the week since the metal safe, he has uploaded new content daily. Somehow, each video more interesting than the last. Military dog tags, a real Rolex, two hand guns, even an antique dagger. I tap on the notification and the latest one plays. Gold coins! Okay, I'm highly suspicious that he's faking these finds for views. I can't blame him, it's a lot of effort for little payoff. It hasn't made a difference, though, because his follower count is only at 47. Can he see that I view his account dozens of times a day? Hm…

My phone vibrates, Ivy's face fills the screen.

"Hey sis!"

"Hey Bug. I'm on lunch break eating Jimmy's, thinking of you"

"Ugh, gloat much? You know I'd kill for a hand pie right now."

"Haha sorry. How's work?"

"Uh, working from bed today, super productive."

"You getting outside? Vitamin D!"

"...yes?"

"Sammy..."

"I'm doing my best, Ivy."

"I know. Sorry."

"So...how are you? What's new?"

"Eh, boring old Quincy. Oh! There's been a rash of burglaries. Jack's paranoid about his Chevelle"

"I'm sure they don't want his rusty old car frame...wait, how many burglaries?"

"Maybe half a dozen. Why?"

I tell Ivy about MagMan, leaving out how much time I spend gawking at his account. She feigns interest while sprinkling in reminders to put my phone away at night, go outside in the morning, and make a follow-up with Dr. Reed. I assure her I'm on top of things while steering the conversation back to my suspicions.

"Sammy, if this guy is the burglar, I'm sure the cops will figure it out."

"Are you suggesting I put my trust in Quincy PD?"

"I...sorry Sam, no."

"Gotta go, Ivy. Love you, enjoy lunch"

***

I climb into bed with a hot cup of tea and slice of toast. Not a hand pie, but all I'm motivated to prepare. I hate lying to Ivy, but if I told her that I was in bed scrolling instead of working, she'd probably call Dr. Reed herself.

I pull up police blotters for Quincy and surrounding towns, seeking evidence to support my suspicions.

TRAFFIC STOP - NO ARREST

DISTURBANCE - REPORTED

BURGLARY - REPORTED

LOUD MUSIC - COULD NOT LOCATE

DOMESTIC - UNFOUNDED

BURGLARY - REPORTED

Not enough detail in the blotters. I scour newspapers and local Facebook groups. A pattern unfolds. In the last six months, four people have vanished from four of the small towns surrounding Quincy. In each case, personal belongings were also missing. I find the Facebook profile for one of the missing - David, age 44 from Enosburg. Collector of antique weapons. The dagger MagMan found flashes in my mind.

Nah.

I dig through David's profile, heart pounding with each tap of the screen. I freeze, my breath seizing in my lungs.

There it is. The dagger.

I open my contacts and tap Ivy's face.

"Hey, finishing up at wo—"

"Ivy, listen to me. I was right. It's worse than I thought"

I hastily explain everything I've seen, my voice quivering with fear and desperation. Ivy is silent as I lay out the details of my theory.

"Bug…did you work today?"

Fuck. She's not taking me seriously. I try my best to steer her back to my concerns.

"Sammy, I'm worried about you. I know this time of year is hard, but maybe with the anniversary of…"

"That's not it!"

"When was the last time you left the house?"

"Please listen to me"

"I love you, Sammy. You're getting lost in conspiracy theories. I'm going to call Dr. Reed. Then I'm coming to stay with you. Please, put the phone away. Go for a walk."

I deflate with a sigh of defeat. She thinks I'm crazy. Maybe she's right.

***

I have been lying here for 20 minutes staring at my ceiling, willing myself to move. It's not happening. I open Dr. Reed's contact, thumb hovering over the call button. Instead, I quickly change apps and open MagMan's profile. I stare in contemplation for several seconds. With sweaty palms, I swipe through each video, hoping he revealed himself and I missed it.

My doom scrolling is interrupted by a text from Ivy.

'Hey sis, Dr. Reed tomorrow at 12. Gonna pack then hit the road so I can be there, prob arrive by midnight. Bringing hand pies ;). Love you.'

She's too good to me. We're only two years apart, but when mom was murdered, she instinctively took on more than any teen should. She's right. I know she is. The walls of this room have been closing in on me for weeks. I roll out of bed and stand in front of the mirror. I haven't showered in days and it shows…and smells. She can't see me like this.

I scurry around, tossing clothes into laundry baskets, trash into grocery bags, and changing month old linens. For the first time in weeks, I open curtains and blinds fully, allowing what remains of the day's dwindling sunlight to pour over me. Wind picks up, lifting leaves from branches in a whirlwind of color; a smile forms at the corners of my mouth. When did I last smile? Feeling prepared for Ivy, I get lost in a long hot shower.

With fresh clothes, clean sheets, and the comfort of knowing my sister is coming I fall, finally, into a deep sleep.

***

Ow. I rub my eyes and reduce the brightness on my phone. Holy shit, it's almost midnight. I call Ivy. No answer. I check our texts - the last message at 7 PM, saying she was leaving. She should be pulling in any minute now. Ivy is a notoriously safe driver, to an annoying degree. I'm sure she's focused.

PING!

MagMan has gone live for the first time! Tap now to join.

Impulsively, I tap to join. My screen is nearly black, with the faint impression of shadows moving in darkness. A burst of light settles into a steady spotlight illuminating a familiar scene. Craven Bridge. The one that started this whole obsession. He walks up to the rope and begins pulling, gloved hand over gloved hand. Is he moving in slow motion? The magnet creates a splash when breaking the surface of the water. Tension builds wildly in my gut. He remains focused on his hands, never glancing below. A montage of videos, police blotters, missing person's reports, and Facebook photos flashes through my mind. Dripping with sweat, paralyzed, I can't look away. What is he doing?

Carefully he lifts the magnet into view. The light reflects off of something dangling. Something gold. A necklace? Ripples of dread surge upwards from the pit of my gut. A locket.

A heart shaped emerald.

For When You Want Something Special

Clive Wallis

Writer | Chocolate Candies

It was toward the end of the sixth month that he got the box down from the cupboard. Six months of nothing. Six months of staring at a cursor. Six months of starting, then stopping, then jamming his finger hard on the back-space key until all his idiotic dribble was erased and there was just a blank screen again.

He sat the box on the shelf above his desk. He caught himself glancing upwards every few minutes but there it stayed. A small red and black box, perhaps an inch square on one end by five inches long. It was as bright and fresh as the day he'd bought it. It sat at first like an invitation, then like a warning. By the middle of the seventh barren month it felt like a reproach.

On the first Monday of the eighth month, he moved the box down to his desk, ignoring how his fingers trembled. Still he wrote nothing.

That night he dreamt he was back in the market in Cambodia. He was standing in front of the old man again, everything around him seeming to fade away just as it had fourteen years ago. He met the old man's bright blue eyes again, only this time he shook his head no. This time his hand didn't reach for his wallet but instead came up in front of his face, palm facing out, like a cop stopping traffic. *No.* He woke up crying.

***

On Tuesday morning he rolled his chair right up to his desk and picked the box up. Gentle as he was, he felt the thin cardboard bend beneath his fingers and heard the soft sigh of the tissue paper inside. He lowered his thumb nail into the gap and eased up the lid. Four empty spaces stared up at him, the small white cocoons of tissue paper the colour of bleached bone. In the fifth and final space rested a single chocolate, deep brown and lightly dusted in cocoa powder. And that smell. Saliva flooded his mouth. Jasper knew that after fourteen years it shouldn't look or smell so fresh. He laughed; a guttural laugh that was almost a bark. How the fucking things stayed fresh so long really was the least of his worries. He fumbled the lid shut again, spun his chair away from his desk and wheeled himself into the kitchen. He needed to wash his hands. And he needed coffee.

Fourteen years ago he was living in a freezing cold, two-room shoebox, spending eight hours a day pretending to care about insurance and then spending four hours an evening trying to finish his first book. When the insurance company finally fired him, he packed his manuscript and the few summer clothes he owned and got on the first plane headed somewhere hot. Cambodia.

One chocolate and two months later he had an agent. A short while after that he had a three-book deal. Eighteen months after that someone gave him a stupid amount of money for the film rights.

And right after that came the first piece of bad luck. His brand-new house and pretty much everything he owned burnt to a cinder. The fire service said they couldn't recall a blaze of such ferocity. All he got away with was half the contents of his kitchen. Some pots and pans, a cupboard of groceries. And the chocolates.

His agent and his publisher and the journalists and everyone else put the writer's block that followed down to the shock of the fire. And so did Jasper for a while. That was before the second chocolate.

He'd drunk two cups of coffee, sat in the kitchen, lost in thought. He remembered what the old man had said, remembered it like the pop songs of his youth, word for word, effortlessly and completely. "These are very special chocolates. Make them last. Save them for when you want something special." For a long time, he'd wondered at the meaning of that last sentence. But now he knew. Oh yes, he knew.

He was drunk when he ate the second chocolate, and he was drunk for most of the two years after his second book sold even more copies and made him even more money than the first one had. But then came the reckoning. Yes, there was a global financial meltdown towards the end of those two glorious years. Yes, a lot of people lost a lot of money. But something had conspired against Jasper again. He didn't lose a lot of money: he lost it all. A plague of locusts couldn't have done it better. After two bestsellers and two blockbuster film adaptations, he was back in a rented flat and living off his next advance.

Jasper put the coffee cup down and wheeled himself back to his desk. He laid his fingers across the keys, took a deep breath and started to type. Two hours later he had a thousand words. He thought half of them might be worth keeping. He saved the document and shut the laptop down.

***

That night he dreamt Carol was still alive. They had been in bed. She had slipped out and he had followed her into the kitchen. He couldn't have been more than a few seconds behind her, but he was too late. Even with her back to him, he knew what she had done before she turned around. There were great smears of chocolate across the remnants of her mouth. Her skin hung off her bones like scraps of torn newspaper. The empty sockets of her eyes sucked all the light out of the room. "I'm afraid I've finished your chocolates," she said.

Charles, his nurse, heard the screams and was at his bedside in seconds.

"It's okay, it's okay," Jasper whispered, eyes still squeezed shut. "Bad dream. Nightmare. Bad dream."

An hour later, when it was clear that neither of them were going to get back to sleep, Charles helped him shower and dress and get into his chair. It was still dark. Jasper watched in grateful silence as Charles moved from lamp to lamp and small pools of soft light pushed the shadows away.

He'd eaten the third chocolate in full knowledge of what was to come. He'd tried again for months and months but all he had was a few thousand decent words and the barest, stilted outline that could have been a grocery list. His agent was growing less cajoling and more irritated with each phone call. He ate the third chocolate and waited, and it came, just like it had before. The words flowed. Less than before but still enough. And it was damn good.

Sometimes, Jasper thought the year or so that followed was the best time of his life. He and Carol travelled, partied, laughed, even danced sometimes. But he knew he was kidding himself. The best time of his life was way back; back when he was unpublished. Back before Cambodia. Before he bought the chocolates.

This time he didn't lose his house or his money. Carol came home one day from the doctor's and before she said a word he knew. He knew by the set of her shoulders, the grey hue of her face, the fear in her eyes. It was May, his favourite time of year. She was dead before the leaves started to turn. A battalion of expensive doctors said they'd never seen cancer so aggressive, couldn't explain it. Jasper thought he could.

He ate the fourth chocolate a week after the funeral. What would turn out to be his prize-winning fourth novel poured out of him in torrents. It was short, shorter even than the last one, virtually a novella, but what did that matter? He was hot again.

He'd only had the fancy German sports car a week and of course that was a suitable explanation, for those who needed one. He had no memory of the crash at all, just a blank page. He remembered leaving the house. Then nothing until waking up in the hospital. His first thought wasn't what happened? *or* where am I? *or even* why can't I feel my legs? *His first thought was* I'm alive. Bring it on, you motherfucker, whoever or whatever you are. I'm alive and I've still got one chocolate left.

Easier to remember that moment than the fifteen months of pain and pills and operations and physical therapy that followed. Were there times when he thought about swallowing an entire box of meds and washing it down with a bottle of vodka? Too many to count. But somehow, he kept going. Until now.

He felt a hand on his arm and almost threw his coffee in his lap. "Sorry Jasper," said Charles. "I've got to pop out. Your pills." He waved a prescription apologetically in his other hand. Jasper looked up. It was daylight. The sun laid bright stripes on the carpet.

"Sure," he said. "No hurry. Bring me back a latte and something sweet. I'm going to look over yesterday's draft."

Jasper waited for the click of the key in the lock before wheeling himself over to his desk. As his laptop booted up, he opened the chocolate box. There it was. One last little treat. He plucked it out of its paper nest and stuffed it in his mouth before he could change his mind. This time his hands were sure and steady. The taste was, as ever, exquisite. Sweet, but a little note of something bitter. *The really bitter part is still to come,* he thought. In seconds the chocolate was gone. He deleted yesterday's document and pulled up a blank page.

This is what happened, he wrote. Not great, but as suicide notes go, he thought it was a better start than *I'm sorry* or *Know that I love you.* His fingers danced over the keys, the words coming quick and smooth, like running water. He felt it somewhere deep in his mind; a kernel of energy, a burning mote of force, the words coming and coming.

They were still flooding out of him when the first drop of blood hit the keyboard. Jasper ran the back of his hand across his nostrils and carried on typing. Eyes fixed on the screen, he didn't see the dark swathe of red across his hand, fresh and vivid as a stroke of paint. Another drop fell, and another. He sniffed hard and wiped his nose again. This time he did see his hand as he placed it back on the keyboard. It was a thick wet glove of blood.

"Fuck you," he told the chocolate box.

He awkwardly wiped the back of his hand down the side of his sweatshirt and resumed typing. Now he could feel the blood running across his lips. It fell from his chin in a thick crimson waterfall that pattered onto the keys. Still he kept typing. Not long now. Almost finished. Then he noticed his hands.

There was blood on his fingers, blood between them, smears of it all over the keyboard. It was easing out from under his fingernails. As he stared transfixed, his left index and middle fingers split open, blood spurting up onto the laptop screen. The four fingers of his right hand tore apart. He screamed as the skin and muscle peeled back up to his knuckles. Coils of skin flapped uselessly like strips of red apple peel. He brought both hands up in front of his face. Bone shone red where his fingers and thumbs should be. He screamed again. He was still screaming when first his left and then his right eye dissolved into orbs of blood. It splattered so thick and dark onto his keyboard that it looked almost brown. Brown and smooth, almost the colour of chocolate.

The Friends We Keep

Ana Nelson

Mycologist | Empty Pockets

"This is it," Juniper said as she slammed her car door shut and looked around. She hadn't been to her childhood home in twenty years. Cooper stepped out of the driver's side and stretched before surveying the house.

"It's smaller than I pictured it."

"Disappointed already?" She snapped back, but if he noticed her tone, he ignored it.

"Of course not. The real treasure is inside, as long as you weren't exaggerating. Kids, you know."

"I'm not sure why you think this house will be special."

"I don't, really," he said, pulling his giant bag of lab equipment out of the car. "But even if it wasn't as unique as you remember, which it probably wasn't, the conditions in this area are perfect. It's always damp, it's super humid in the summer. I'm just excited to see what grows without worrying about work."

"Well, I just hope you won't mope around the whole time if it's not what you're expecting."

"I won't mope if you don't," he said, hoisting his bags and heaving them up the front steps. He entered the house with Juniper close behind. The old steps seemed to sink under her feet and she was surprised they didn't snap under her weight. She entered the house and closed the door behind them.

***

When Juniper was young, she found a Tupperware full of mold in the back of the fridge. Her mom had taken one look at it and gasped before snatching it from Juniper's hands and marching out of the kitchen.

"Jerold! Why is the lunch I made for you three weeks ago still in the fridge?!" she'd screeched, waving the container in front of his nose. He'd just frowned and looked at her.

"I don't know. Sorry, dear." He mumbled, looking down at his loafers. Juniper watched from the door frame until her mother's tirade had subsided. Then she snuck up to her father's armchair and whispered up at him, making sure mama couldn't hear.

"What is it, dad? Where did it come from?"

"Mold grows on food sometimes when it goes bad."

"It grows? Like me?"

"Even faster than you."

"Is it alive?"

"…I guess so," he said after a moment.

She was amazed. It was alive. The next day, she didn't eat her sandwich. She hid it in her backpack and tucked it in the back of her closet after school. And every day she would check on it, waiting. It only took four days for the little blue spots to start sprouting from the pores in her sandwich. Throughout the week, the blue expanded into white and gray, until she couldn't tell where the sandwich stopped and the mold began.

"Mom called me stupid yesterday," she told it, opening the lid and stroking the fluff with the tip of her finger. "But Ms. Johnson said she liked my paper." She told it all about her day, about school, what rocks she found at recess, and all the things her mom told her she did wrong that day.

"Sometimes I hate her," she whispered, before snapping the blue plastic lid closed and putting it back in the closet, happy to know it was there, just waiting for the next time she would open it.

***

Cooper set his lab up in her old bedroom. He pushed all her childhood trinkets to the side of her dresser and set up a microscope. Soon, there were just as many petri dishes as there were figurines. He hadn't bothered to ask before shoving her old things aside.

There had been no signs of mold beyond what was normal for an old, neglected house. Cooper Hadn't left her childhood room the entire day.

"I want to go out to eat," she told him that evening, standing in the doorway with her arms crossed. He didn't even look up from his sample.

"Don't you think we've already spent enough on gas and food on the way up here? I thought you wanted to relax in the country."

"So you're just going to sit in here alone the whole time?"

"It's only been a day. I don't know why we came here at all if you're going to be like this," he said, swapping out the slide and flipping to a different lense. She stood in the doorway for a while, staring at the harsh line of his jaw as he clenched his teeth, before retreating to the living room alone.

***

Juniper fed her friend every day when she got home. She would drop carrots and grapes in the container before sprinkling a little water on top.

"Here you go, I know you're thirsty," she would say, petting it and leaving some parts flattened under her hand. She didn't bother with the lid anymore. The mold had stretched thin, white tendrils up to the lip of the container, then over, spreading across the floor like a fuzzy white spider's web.

She would stay in the closet until she heard her mom's unsteady footsteps marching down the hallway. Her mom would fling the door open and lean down in front of her, breath sickly sweet, and ask her why she was so messy, so awkward, and if her homework was done, why her bed wasn't made, and if her bed was made, Juniper would have to listen to her cry and tell her what a deadbeat dad was. And when her dad would walk down the hallway towards the bathroom, and they would lock eyes, she would plead with him silently, *Tell her I'm OK, tell her to go to bed*, but he would look away guiltily and she would hear the lock slide into place on the bathroom door. When her mom would finally leave, she would crawl into the closet and hold the container, feeding it salty tears.

***

"Look, I found something!" Cooper said when he finally left her bedroom at midnight. Juniper ignored him, staring at the TV, her face set to a scowl. "C'mon... I know you want to see," he said, sliding over to her on the couch and putting his hand on her thigh.

"Oh, now you want to talk?" She said, crossing her legs and swatting his hands away. Instantly, she saw the light drain from his eyes and felt the air in the room shift.

"You always do this. Nag at me to not bring the mood down, and then you're the one that ruins it."

"I—"

"Whatever. I don't want to fight. I'm going to get more samples." He stood from the couch and went back to her old bedroom, to the closet still brimming with mold, and she was glad. She stared up at the ceiling, wondering how things could be so different while still being exactly the same. There was mold in the corner that she hadn't seen before, little black speckles making their way across the walls.

***

It wasn't long before the mold grew too big for Juniper to hide. It spilled out from under the crack in her closet door, crawling up her dressers and wrapping around her dolls until they were white and fuzzy. Her mother was furious. But no matter how many times her parents cleaned the house from top to bottom, it was back the next day. Eventually, they gave up, and the mold became a normal part of life. Juniper was thrilled. Her friends were everywhere. The walls of her bedroom were so coated that it looked like black and blue polka dotted wallpaper. She still talked to the container the most. A multicolored spongy mold had absorbed the container, and little black mushrooms had sprouted from the top, with stems as thin as hairs. She cradled it in her arms and whispered to it.

"I hate them. I wish they weren't here."

We're here for you, it seemed to say, *we'll help.* And she believed them. The next morning when she looked into her mother's eyes, her pupils were cloudy and milky white, just like the newly born mold on the kitchen curtains.

***

The next day, Juniper let Cooper show her the slides of the mold. But she couldn't make herself listen as he told her about it. Something about rapid growth and a massive number of fused mycelia.

"Babe, are you even listening?"

No, she thought.

"What was that?" She said instead. He gave her a look and sighed.

"Anyway, look what I found this morning..." He said, digging through his pockets. "Huh, that's odd." He pulled his coat pockets inside out. They were both empty. Instead, mold had weaved its way into the thin fabric of his coat, reaching for his skin. He took it off and stared at it before running back into her bedroom. Slowly, Juniper followed. Cooper was on her bed, petri dishes spread around him in a circle, his hands full of mold. She crept towards the closet. Sure enough, when she opened the door, her container was there, with a shriveled orange ball of mold inside. The ball was warm when she held it in her hand, soft and familiar, an old friend.

***

Juniper noticed several changes in her parents. Her mom had little purple spots on her fingernails that spread up her hand and were bumpy to the touch. Her father's eyes had clouded over so much that you couldn't tell where his pupils were. He barely moved anymore. Mostly he sat in his rocking chair, and if he wasn't yawning, he was coughing. He stopped going to work. Mom was in the kitchen. She sat at the table, staring down into her cup of water, watching the little clumps bobbing around inside. She couldn't move either. Thick tendrils coated her arms and wrapped around both her legs and the chairs, tying them together. Her hand was outstretched towards where the phone lay just out of reach.

"Jun... iper," she wheezed. Juniper knew what she wanted. She even thought about calling for help. But when she looked into her mother's eyes and saw the anger there, she didn't want to pick up the phone. Instead, she walked quietly away, every step she took sending spores flying up into the air.

***

Cooper had been so excited he hadn't even noticed the light fading outside the window, and she hadn't bothered to tell him. The mold had returned to the walls, just like before, and she smiled at the comforting, familiar pattern. The spots seemed to wink at her in the shifting light; *we're still here, we remember.* The mold had coated the entire floor, even thicker than the carpet, and she felt it seep between her toes as she walked. Cooper was still sprawled out on her bed, surrounded by little samples of mushroom and mold, but as she got closer, she saw he wasn't sleeping. He was staring up at the ceiling with wide horrified eyes, his breathing fast and shallow. All over his skin, the purple spots had wormed their way into his body. Soon, he would be just like her parents had been, covered in a fuzzy white burial shroud. In just a few days, he would be completely devoured. She leaned forward, looking into his eyes.

"What's wrong? I thought you liked fungus." She said, relishing in the fear, finally in his eyes instead of her own. In the morning, she would leave. But for now, she held the little orange ball of mold to her chest and closed her eyes, listening.

We're here.

It's OK.

You can leave him with us.

We know you'll be back someday.

What Did They Do to You?

Victoria Higgins

Call Centre Worker | A Blindfold

The work is at unsociable hours, but that's just fine with me. I don't sleep well these days anyway. Don't socialise much either. Every other night I take the bus to the city centre, walk over to a tall brick office building. A security guard, Gary, meets me at the entrance and swipes a card to let me in. The glass doors open with a swoosh. It's swanky inside, with shiny tables dotted around the lobby like freshly iced cakes. Gary takes me up to the 5th floor in the lift. It always smells like plaster up there. We walk through the hall, past rows of empty unfinished offices. I'm led to the end of the hall where there's a small room with a chair and a table. At the side there's a great hulking machine twinkling with colourful lights and hooked up to it is my headphone and microphone set, sat waiting for me on the table.

Once I've sat down, Gary puts the hood over my head. It only covers my eyes like the ones they use on birds of prey. I don't know why he doesn't just let me put it on myself, but there you go.

It was annoying at first, the blindfold thing, because I had to learn the script off by heart. I hadn't memorised anything since school and I've not exactly treated my brain well since then. It took me three whole days, just sat in that room repeating line after line until I got it right. The management were decent about it though, I was told I could have all the time I needed.

It's like that in a lot of call centres, the managers are desperate to keep you because they're totally haemorrhaging people, you can get away with basically anything. I've worked in some nasty ones too, where they're recruiting people out of half-way houses to scam little old ladies over the phone. To be honest I thought this job would be like that as well when I first heard about it, cash-in-hand and covert and all that. Maybe I am scamming people to be fair. I don't really know what I'm doing.

After I'm blindfolded, I hear Gary leave. Maybe he waits outside and watches me through the slit windows in the door. I'm wearing a headset, but the voices don't come to me through the earpiece. No, they burst out from within my brain, like a reptile breaking out of an eggshell. Really it's like they're calling me, but if they speak at all they always go first like they're picking up the phone. *Hello? Hello?* That rising intonation, hopeful or apprehensive, as though they've been waiting for me to call.

How are you today? That's always the first question, simple enough. And the script says that no matter what the person says, you have to respond: *that's good, I'm well thank you.*

Then you ask, *what do you see?* Surprisingly, a lot of the time people turn that back on you. The script takes care of that though, because then you answer that you can see absolutely nothing. Most of the time that calms people down because their answer is the same. Sometimes they tell me something kind of beautiful: the silhouette of a single tree against a charcoal black sky, craning up to reach the lightning; the dead light of a fluorescent lamp illuminating a bouquet of flowers. Stuff like that.

Eventually: *what did they do to you?* That one can really get people going. If they answer at all, if they're not just whimpering or wailing or laughing, people will tell you some pretty gruesome stories. I won't repeat anything here, but let's just say I've done call centre work for a personal injury firm and these stories are a lot worse.

They're pretty strict about that rule, keeping to the script. The first time I did one of these calls - or should I say the first time someone spoke to me, because a lot of the time you get through to someone and you can feel that they are there, but they don't say anything, so let's say the first time I spoke to someone - I asked how they were and they wouldn't stop bleating "*is Margie there? Where's Margie?*" on and on and so I thought, it doesn't make sense to say *that's good, I'm well thank you,* and so I told them that no, she wasn't there. They hung up then, and everything was fine, but that morning I came home to a letter slipped under my door that read:

Dear Employee,

FORMAL WARNING

As you are aware, deviation from the script is a violation of the employee Code of Conduct and will not be tolerated. Please consider this letter as notification of your first formal warning. If this incident reoccurs, this will be treated as a serious disciplinary matter. If you require more information or a refreshment on the company rules, please consult your Employee Manual.

Kind regards,
Mr Wye

So I didn't do it again after that, even though the script doesn't always make much sense.

That might seem strict, but it's nothing compared to the blindfold rule. They really drilled that into me during my training, there's a zero-tolerance policy for lifting your hood during a call, that's an instant dismissal or even worse. And I don't know if you can tell, but I really need this job. There's not many places that will hire someone like me, with a record like mine. And even if I could get a job at another call centre, or a warehouse, or wherever, I can't much stand being around people since it happened. People make me itchy, with their eyes and their hands and their mouths constantly moving and shifting like beetles.

Have I ever wanted to take the blindfold off? Well, when you do these calls, it's not like a normal phone call, I know that. The air changes, it gets heavier. Sometimes it feels like that person's voice has clawed its way out of my head and they are there, body and voice, sat right in front of me. There's a smell that comes with that feeling, sulphurous. Of course I want to see if anything's there, but I don't think I'd like it.

Towards the end of a call, you have to ask *how can we help you?* Most of the time the answers are meaningless. Frantic requests to find such and such person, go to such and such place. Maybe someone is listening and they're going to answer these garbled requests, maybe that's the point of all this. It definitely won't be me.

When I was working in normal call centres, I got the idea into my head that one day I might hear her voice down the end of the line. You speak to so many people, day after day, there's got to be a decent chance that one day you'll come across someone you know. That's what I thought. While the line was ringing out I would imagine her voice coming through, bright and clear, wondered if she would recognise mine. Stupid obviously.

The thing is, I was in a bad place when I got this job. I've been in a bad place for a while. I was seeing her more and more. There was nothing for a long time, right after it happened. I was numb, like my head was stuffed with cotton wool. Sure, there was the occasional time when I stopped breathing, when it felt like my insides were on fire. But mostly I was okay, I didn't *see* her. It wasn't until about a year later, after I'd been inside that she started popping up everywhere. Out of the corner of my eye there she was, on the bus, in the supermarket, dank matted hair, gaunt and grey with her mouth open and black like a kid had scribbled it out with biro. And I knew that must have been her mouth that night, wide and screaming down the phone to me, her breathing ragged. The call cut out, and I tried ringing her back again and again but of course she didn't answer. Part of me knew later, when I saw in the newspaper that they'd dredged up a woman from the river. I fully knew when they reported on the inquest, the story smattered with details from the toxicology report. I won't let anyone tell me not to blame myself.

I have this reoccurring dream about her. I'm walking along the river and I feel a buzz next to my ear that makes me flinch. And when I turn around she's there, so many meters below me, her white face straining above the water, almost submerged, her eyes and mouth leaking. And I'm shouting down at her, *who did this to you? What did they do to you?* And her mouth opens wider and wider until her face is crumbling with the force of it, but she can't utter a word.

And when I started doing this job I did think, maybe one of these days I really will hear her.

One day, I'll hear that voice. I'll feel the presence first, smell that sulphurous smell and know someone is on the other end.

So I say it. *How are you today?* Drop those words into the cavern, and then like a bird swooping up from the deep I'll hear her. "*John?*" she says. My heart lurches. My mouth fills with sand.

"*John, I've missed you so much.*" Her voice is so warm, radiant. I think about lying in bed next to her, playing video games with her, laughing. "*How are you?*"

I freeze. I don't know what to say and so, stupidly, I follow the script. "*That's good, I'm well thank you,*"

Her voice breaks then, she starts to whimper.

"*John, I'm so scared,*" she says, "*I don't know where I am. It's so dark here, I'm so cold.*"

I feel it then, a shiver slices through me like a knife, the hair on my arms stands to attention. She's really crying now, heaving with sobs.

"*John, you won't believe what they did to me. They hurt me so badly, I can't even tell you. Why did you make me go to that horrible place? Please, John, please listen to me now.*"

There's a glass bubble expanding in my throat, I can't speak or it'll shatter. I become aware of the fact that she is there, very close to me, right next to my face. I can smell the sweet smell of her, sweat and body lotion, the brine of her breath.

"*You have to help me John, please, after everything you did please help me now. I'm so lonely and I'm so scared. All I'm asking is that you look at me, you're always looking away from me John, you're always turning away. Please just look at me. You won't believe what they did to me.*"

The salty smell of her breath is stronger now, dank and overpowering, brushing against my hood like a sea breeze. She's begging me, she won't stop, to take it off. I know immediately that I'll do it, the rules be damned, that's my dead girlfriend after all.

I also know that what awaits me on the other side is awful, that the rules must be there for a reason. But I lift my hood and I let her pull me into the darkness.

Out of Mind

Nicoletta Giuseffi

Self Help Guru | A Strange Proposal

Another canvas ruined by indecision. The paint had dried, leaving blotches of ugly, half-formed colors. Although it caught a bright square of morning peeking in through the blackout curtain, Radha only saw its flaws, which where inchoate but certainly predestined. This canvas was foretelling her failure, her destruction, and the desolation of her artistic ability. Walls were closing in. She'd be on the street in a few months, or facing a degrading minimum wage job, or worse: she'd be forced to lower herself to the same level as other artists like her, pumping out fan art for the algorithm and never getting to tell her story.

With a cry, Radha dashed the canvas to the floor. The easel collapsed like the structure of her mind which held her art aloft and out of reach most days. Intrusive thoughts told her to burn it, but she had no fireplace. The same voice told her there was no escape from her downward spiral. The realization appeared before her like blood blooming on white linen: she had wasted her education, shackled herself to loans, and all for a mediocre talent. Nothing of note. She fell to her knees and beat her fists on the carpet until her bones ached.

A knock sounded at the door and with a full-body cringe, Radha recalled her fussy downstairs neighbor Miranda. For a moment she considered pretending she wasn't there.

"Radha? Are you alright? I heard a crash, did something fall?"

Radha opened the door in a ratty t-shirt and black sleep shorts, her legs pale against the fluorescent hall lights. There was Miranda, a well put-together woman of an imposing height, wearing black gloves and a coat with a faux-fur trim. She pushed a fringe of her bob behind her ear and one of her earrings, a golden branch, bounced against her neck. Her face reminded Radha of her mother's.

"I'm fine. Sorry about the noise."

The bags under Radha's eyes must have betrayed her anguish, because Miranda scoffed and shifted her leg so the toe of her boot sat inside the doorway.

"Do you know what I do?"

"You're a life coach or something? I don't know. I don't go to the complex-wide mixers anymore."

"You're half right. Radha, I don't usually do this, but I hate seeing a sweet young face so torn by sadness. And I hate loud noises in the morning. Normally I charge what I'm worth, but I think I can help you very easily, and even gain something from it."

"A quiet neighbor?"

Miranda laughed like a bell chiming and placed her hand on the doorframe.

"A happy neighbor. Ignore me if you like, send me away, but once you hear my proposal, I think you'll be quite interested. I'm more than a life coach. I'm an expert. A master of my trade. I can rid you of every negative thought plaguing that pretty head. You'll never have to suffer another tear. Never another dark spiral of guilt keeping you up until the wee hours. You're an artist, so I expect your craft will come easier, too."

Radha stared blearily for a moment, swallowed, and removed the chain on the door.

"Come in."

"It won't take long," Miranda drawled, tugging off her left glove and following Radha into the haphazard studio apartment crowded with half-finished canvases and dried palettes.

"Sorry, hang on." Radha crouched in front of the sofa and gathered up a pile of dark clothes reeking of midnight sweat. She moved them to a chair and then offered Miranda a seat next to her.

Miranda settled as gracefully as a hummingbird landing on a flower stem, but her dark eyes pierced like the beak into nectar.

"I can help you. I've helped many before. You have bad thoughts, and doctors tell you it's chemical, yes? But you've tried a half-dozen pills of questionable nomenclature, combinations, homeopathic remedies, prayer, meditation, oh, Radha, what haven't you tried?"

"Nothing," Radha sighed, cradling her elbows. More negative thoughts were already flooding in, but this time they warned of danger. Was she really becoming so antisocial that she couldn't talk to her own neighbor? A friendly single woman just like her, give or take a few decades. Maybe it had been harder for Miranda when she was first starting out, too.

No, that was ridiculous. Everything had gotten harder after two recessions.

Miranda reached out and took Radha's hand with her uncovered one. Despite the wrinkles around her eyes, Miranda's hand was softer and smoother than Radha's, where dry, cracked knuckles and bitten nails reflected a prisoner in a deep oubliette clawing against a stone wall. The fingers were so soft Radha was struck by the idea they had no prints, but she wasn't so impolite as to check. She allowed Miranda to cup her hand, to thread fingers, and when she was done and her hand was gone, she missed its warmth. Maybe human contact was all she really needed.

"Now," Miranda said, "it is done. Let me teach you a trick. This should be easy—you've got such long, beautiful hair. The next time you have a bad thought, you'll feel it like a nail in your head. Since that's no place for nails, I want you to draw it out. Find the hair closest to it and pull. You'll feel the difference immediately."

Before Miranda had finished speaking, Radha was wincing, closing one eye as a sharp, electric pain crackled inside her scalp. Rather than a nebulous headache, it was a singing, definite point, and she could barely resist setting both hands on her head and searching for the hair closest to the pain. When she found it, she separated it and plucked it out. There was a gentle pop, then an immense feeling of relief. Something came with it, perhaps the root, so she held it in front of her face to examine it. There was something dangling there at the end. A tiny, smooth, grey grub.

"That can't be normal," Radha whispered. The feeling of calm washing over her precluded any sort of disgusted reaction. The coin of her mind had flipped, and now tails were heads, and bad thoughts were sweet suppositions about rain in the sun and a warm croissant enjoyed on the fire escape.

"It's perfectly normal. All I ask is that you keep those hairs you pluck. Keep them like a bouquet, or a precious artifact from a lover or an ancestor."

"The Victorians made hair wreaths."

"I know," Miranda said, smiling nicotine and slipping her hand back into her glove. "I'll come back in a while to check on you. I have a speaking engagement, so I'll be going now. Remember: bad thoughts are just little spots on the window pane, aphids in the garden, maggots on the rot. Rid yourself of them and thrive."

***

Radha wrapped another hair around the wooden stake in a ceramic pot whose occupant was long-dead. A smile spread over her face. There was a sizeable bundle of hairs now, and the bulbous ends crowded against each other like seed pods. She examined them, marveling at how these bad thoughts were so small, so harmless by themselves. It was in her head that they caused all the damage, becoming a deluge of negativity which sapped her energy and stifled her creativity until it was as frayed as she was. But she wasn't frayed anymore. She was thriving.

Her computer screen looked so different with the curtains drawn and the sun coming in. She couldn't remember the last time she greeted the day with yoga and food, real food, instead of just coffee. While she glanced at her notifications, she licked jam and flakes of croissant from her fingers. Her latest piece was a huge success online, and a few people even reached out to her offering illustration work. Someone else, from a publication following art and social media, had contacted her for a statement about the piece. It was one thing looking at her photos of it on the screen, but she hadn't been able to keep from gazing lovingly at the canvas nearby like a proud mother.

Radha convinced herself she had painted it while in a fugue, or else, she was so blissful she couldn't remember composing the piece and filling in all the details. More than once she woke up on the floor next to the canvas, so she knew she must have worked through the night. Turning away from the painting of a thousand idealized good thoughts bursting from the head of a young woman, Radha checked her metrics again. She did so every hour, but now the likes and praise had begun to slow down.

A sizzle of acute, pinprick pain suddenly burst against her scalp from inside. There must have been someone out there who hated her, who throttled her account, because she had followed all the posting guidelines, said the right keywords, replied to the right commenters, and still the results were subpar. Real art resulted in an unending well of support. She felt her mood deflating and reached up into her hair, where a growing bald spot was the least of her concerns. She tugged on another one, felt it pop out of her scalp, and as she had done for the first hair those weeks ago, she held it in front of her face. The end dangled heavily. Had that big chunk of tissue come from inside her head?

If only she could remember who taught her this trick, she'd thank them from the bottom of her heart. She wrapped the hair around her finger and picked up her phone, thinking of calling her mother to share the news of her success. Happiness had to be shared. Only, she couldn't remember her mother's face. Her fingers danced over her phone's lock screen, but she couldn't remember her password, either. Another miserable moment of misfortune, another hair removed, another smile. Perhaps if she used her phone less, she'd be more consistently happy. Another hair, another, before the pain blinded her. Now she had a bundle on her finger, but she couldn't recall where she had been putting them.

Miranda was standing in the kitchenette with her hand on the counter.

"I'm so sorry," Radha said, "I forgot I was entertaining." Miranda's angular cheeks resembled someone she knew, or once knew, but she didn't know their name. Trying to recall only made her frustrated, and that meant she had to pluck out another hair. This time, it felt like she had plucked out a piece of her brain. It was hanging on the end of the cord of hair, as round and glossy as a marble, with a tiny branch attached below.

"Radha, you're looking well," said a voice hovering beside her. A hand took her chin and lifted it so her eyes were caught inside the dark wells of a tall woman's gaze. She was beautiful, all crimson lips and beaming yellow teeth. "You're almost entirely free of those negative thoughts, aren't you? I'd like to see the hairs. Here they are around your finger. Let's take them over to the others, shall we? There now, we'll gather them into a nice bundle. You found a fitting place for them. These magic little dendrites resemble plants, don't they?"

Radha nodded. She couldn't find the words to respond. A shock of embarrassment rose from the center of her mind to the surface of her scalp, and she automatically tore a chunk of hair from the general area in exchange for an instantaneous balm of happiness. She watched, wordlessly, as the tall woman in black took the hair from her hand and added it to the rest. Then she raised the hairs above her head and dangled the hundreds of fat bits of brain matter over her face. She lowered the bundle into her mouth, closed her lips around it, and began to chew.

In the Dark, Nothing Flowers

David Cotton

CCTV Operator | Bouquet

Si staggered back into the toilet cubicle, hands against his eyes. He heard a strange sound outside as he clawed at the shapes stuck to his face. Pulling the soft leaves away, he could feel his skin peeling away with them.

The room was suddenly dark. Si groped for his torch; fumbling, instead it clattered to the floor. He knelt, feeling wildly for it, ignoring the dead leaves across the tiles.

The overhead lights flicked back on, then off; a towering shape of twisted brown, green and red was momentarily illuminated in the mirrors opposite. He swung up his torch, heart racing, and pressed the button.

A mouth shot forward, clamped around his hand, and dragged him, screaming, from the cubicle.

***

Trish's mother was driving her crazy. She wished she hadn't answered. She'd been driving, and should have told her to piss off. Instead, she'd spent the last twenty minutes listening to how amazing her sister Ellie's fiancé was. How he'd bought Ellie a lovely bouquet of autumn flowers, and wasn't it a shame that Trish hadn't found someone equally thoughtful?

Only two men had ever bought flowers for Trish. First was Stinky Billie, when she was sixteen; those flowers had sat in a vase, slowly rotting, while she vowed to kill him. The second was a terrible blind date with a handsy freak; that huge bunch went straight in the bin.

Mum reminded her that Trish wasn't ladylike enough. Maybe men were threatened by a rugby-playing female security guard. Maybe she could try looking a bit less like a lesbian?

"Mum, I'm at work now," interrupted Trish, parking up. "Love you, bye."

"Let me jus—" Trish pressed the red 'call ending' button with a sigh of relief. She knew Mum meant well. But Trish had tried everything. She seemed to either attract weirdoes or desperate men.

Still, she *would* like to have someone give her flowers.

The rain was hammering. She ran into the hospital entrance.

"Evening, lads!"

Trish entered the office, waiting for the usual banter from the security team, but it was empty. She pulled off her wet North Face jacket, flinging it on the back of the sofa, and walked through the archway to the control room.

"Evening," murmured Jack, whilst chewing on crisps.

"Where's the boys?" Trish glanced at the monitors. Usual chaos in A&E; car parks and corridors empty.

"Si and Flinty were early."

"Early? You've got to be kidding. Those knobheads wouldn't be early to their own funerals!"

Jack snorted. "They came to watch the match." He lifted a green packet. "Crisp?"

"Nah, just had breakfast," replied Trish, leaning on the back of Jack's tall office chair. "What do I need to know?"

"A+E's usual chaos. Bugger all else going on. This rain's keeping most people away."

Jack handed the black hand radio to Trish, who flicked the button. "Radio test, over," she said, her eyes watching the black-and-white monitors as their pictures flicked past.

A voice crackled through. "Mobile two receiving loud and clear, over." The Scottish accent told her it was Flinty.

"Evening, Flinty," she replied. No response.

Jack stood up and stretched. "Think I'll get Chinese tonight. Want me to save you some?"

Trish peered at Jack's large belly. "Will there be any left?"

Jack slugged on his raincoat. "No! Maybe a prawn cracker?"

"Piss off!" She waved him away, then sat in the still-warm swivel chair. On the furthest computer—the one for emails and 'mandatory training'—was an internet page, showing some old photos of buildings.

"Bye!" called Jack, opening the office door.

"Jack, you're logged in."

"Log me out, then?" he asked, disappearing.

The radio was quiet, as were the monitors. Trish swung around to the more colourful computer screen, faintly recognising the pictures. Her eyes ran across the text as she reached for the mouse:

...new hospital building was built on the site of the original Athena Sanitorium, a hospital designed to house the incurable and insane. Ethan Frumen, the occultist, famously wrote that he had attempted to summon a nature spirit in the grounds...

As Trish went to click the window closed, something caught her eye on the main CCTV monitors.

A weird shape had flashed across the screen for a second—racing down an upstairs corridor. She spun the chair around, tapping the controls, pausing the feed and rewinding until she could see it again. Some sort of animal? There was another camera further down, and she flicked it to the central display, but it wasn't shown there. She leaned closer to the image of the original feed, watching it pass in slow motion.

"Trish?" She jumped at the noise from the radio.

"Hey Flinty. You seen Si yet?"

"No. I need help down here. Si's not answering. There's a load of lads kicking off. They've got these weird plants and…"

"I just saw a dog on the CCTV," she interrupted, her voice trembling. The frozen image wasn't anything like a dog.

"Fuck," Flinty cursed. "You'd better go sort that. Where?"

"First floor, near ward sixteen."

"OK. Keep us posted." Flinty's voice was grim.

Trish spun the chair around, ready to get to her feet. "Will d—"

She stopped talking. Sitting in the archway, between the control room and their office slash rest area, was a bunch of flowers.

It was a large bouquet: white roses, lillies, sprigs of green leaves and darker thorns, all carefully arranged. They sat in a dark, wooden vase, carved with intricate patterns of ivy.

"Jack?" she called uncertainly.

Nobody had come in since Jack left. You could hear the electric lock when it activated and deactivated. The two rooms together were barely ten feet long; for someone to have walked in silently and closed the door with flowers still in their hands… it was impossible.

"OK guys, joke's over," Trish said, her voice cracking. She wasn't scared. She'd faced down six-foot men, screaming patients, detoxing addicts. Why was a bunch of flowers making her shiver?

Something made Trish want to stay near the monitors, away from the darker room. She felt behind for the bunch of master keys, trying to keep her eyes on the archway. She cast a quick glance along the desk. The keys were to one side of the smaller monitor. By now, it should have switched onto the password screen, or gone black.

The old writing was still there, the pictures of a building, the words about the Athena Sanitorium visible. But scrawled in front of them, as if written over them in marker on the screen itself, were two words:

THE DARK

The letters were bright red, like fake blood; and they seemed to move as Trish's gaze was drawn towards them, dripping downwards.

Feeling out of control, Trish lunged for the keys, pivoted, and, glancing back at the bunch of flowers, started for the locked door between the control room and the corridor.

Another dark shape flicked past on the CCTV screen. Trish pretended she hadn't noticed. Part of her wanted to radio to Si or Flinty, just to hear a sane voice.

Without warning, there was a sudden, complete darkness.

Trish fell sideways, off balance, and her upper thigh hit the edge of the desk hard. She managed to steady herself, but her heart was pounding. After a second of panic, she realised—*power cut.* Five seconds, and the backup generators would switch on.

It seemed a very long five seconds.

Then there were clicks and fizzes as the TV screens reappeared, displaying their system boot screens. The magnetic door locks clicked back with a 'thunk'. The bar lights flickered, and then settled into their soft glow.

The bouquet had grown.

Trish felt as if she was floating above her head, unable to accept the reality of what she was looking at. Where there had been lilies and roses were now larger, stranger flowers, their red centres growing out into pink, then white; and the straight thorn branches and green leaf surrounds were curled in languid spirals around them.

Trish had had enough. She turned for the door, fumbled the deadlock, then tried to push it open. The door was stuck; after a moment's panic, she remembered the door release button and thumped it, diving through the door and away from the room.

She glanced back in, saw the monitor opposite. It hadn't rebooted; instead, it showed the same internet site with *The Dark* scrawled across it. Only now, there were black tendrils with sharp leaves and small barbs curling across the monitor.

As she registered this, the CCTV cameras flashed back into life, the multiple screens filling with images.

Her radio clicked to life, and then there was a buzz, and a yell. "Help!" The shout was anguished, stopping suddenly, the radio clicking off.

As she heard this noise, she saw a tall man in a shirt—Si?—running across one of the CCTV screens; one arm was limp. Something dark was pursuing him. Suddenly, he fell to the ground and was yanked backwards and out of shot.

Her training was yelling at her to go back into the control room, to rewind and follow the cameras. But her animal, irrational brain was screaming *get the fuck away from this screwed-up insanity*!

She slammed the door. The lights in the corridor were low. She started quickly towards the stairs; then, changing her mind, took a turn towards A+E.

Walking past the men's toilets, she noticed a dark liquid, pooled at one edge of the doorframe.

"Hello?" she asked, pushing gently at the door.

The light inside flickered on. Lying on the floor was a dead man. His face was torn into shreds, bone and muscle visible through the tattered skin. Light brown tendrils covered his body, pushing inside the gaping mouth.

Trish yelped and sprang back, letting the door swing shut again. Hands shaking, she pulled out her radio. "Emergency. Anyone copy?"

Barely waiting, she flicked the switch on top. "Switchboard, do you copy?"

The radio was silent. Trish looked around wildly, waiting for someone or something to appear.

"Fuck!" she hissed, blinking her eyes hard, shaking her head. Then she started running past the dark windows, towards A+E.

Suddenly it was dark again.

Total blackness. Trish could see nothing. There should be small green emergency lights, but it was pitch black.

She groped for her torch and pressed the switch forward. The light was momentarily blinding.

There was a sudden breeze through the corridor, as if a door or window had opened. Trish swung around.

Floating in the air was the bunch of flowers. Leaves and thorns swirled around it; there was a ghostly serpentine shape behind and through it, coiling, ready to spring.

The leaves were the first to hit, flying fast at her. Then a lashing of vines; she swung her arms, trying to rip it all away, and almost succeeded.

Then the flowers were in her face, lit from below by the torch beam. They opened, like a huge mouth, their smell rancid and sweet; and, feeling like soft lips, clamped over her head.

***

Flinty rubbed his eyes. Midnight. He'd finally dragged the four boys out of A+E and cleaned the dirt. He'd lost his radio a while before. He hoped Trish had managed OK on her own.

The corridors were gloomy, but power had reappeared. Despite the light, Flinty didn't see the pooled blood by the men's room door, barely noticed the scattered leaves and petals just beyond.

He opened the door to the security office, saw Trish sitting in the control room swivel chair, staring at the monitors.

"Hey Trish," he mumbled. "That was shit."

The chair swung around. The skin of Trish's face was stripped, tendons and muscle gleaming. Brown tendrils curled into her eye sockets, her nose, her mouth. In her hands, a bunch of white roses and lilies.

"I got you flowers," she croaked.

Unchained

Madeleine Pelletier

Game Developer | Chain Letter

"Unbelievable!" Harriet huffed and threw the newspaper to the ground, sinking back into her mahogany chaise longue. "Unbelievable."

She summoned her maid. "I feel faint."

Cora nodded and left, returning shortly with a tray of sweets.

"Ah, just what I needed." Harriet licked her lips. "I had a terrible turn, you see. After seeing the paper." She paused, waiting, glaring at the maid, and, finally, giving up. "You would not believe what I just read."

"I'm sure you're quite right, ma'am."

"Not a single word about my elegant sociable, is what! Yet Alice's drab soirée received three paragraphs. Can you believe it?" Harriet scoffed, cake crumbs spraying across the green silk in her lap. "An evening of stale crackers and cards. How is that noteworthy?"

"I've no idea, ma'am."

"So what if a Count attended? He's a stuffy old man who can barely stay awake past dinner. And her entertainments? Charades and rhyming games. Neither fancy nor fashionable."

"Sounds awful," said Cora. "Excuse me, ma'am. Postman's here."

Harriet sipped her tea. She was hosting another sociable the following week. Alice was a dear friend. The dearest. But if Harriet's party failed to make the society pages again, Alice would never let her forget it.

"For you, ma'am." Cora placed a postcard next to the teapot.

"I expect it is from my sister, Violet. She has been touring the continent with her husband, the baron."

"Mmm. You mentioned."

"Yes. Fine," Harriet said, annoyed. She picked up the postcard.

> *Oh Lord, I implore thee to bless all mankind. Keep me from evil by thy precious blood and make me to dwell with Thee in Eternity.*
>
> *This is an exact copy of an ancient prayer. She who will not forward it will meet with misfortune, but she who will, for nine days beginning today, send the prayer each day to a friend, will on the ninth day receive great blessings and be delivered from all calamity.*
>
> *Make a wish when writing the prayer and do not be the one to break the chain or catastrophe will follow. It cannot be signed.*

"Humph," said Harriet. "Certainly not from Violet. She would never indulge in such common things. I believe this nonsense is from Alice, attempting to distract me from organizing the perfect party. Well, I will not fall for her ruse." She crumpled the postcard and tossed it in the fire. "Leave me, Cora. I have work to do."

Cora gathered the tea service and left.

Harriet hefted herself up and made her way to her husband's library. She pulled down *The Dictionary of Games and Amusements for Boys and Girls* and flipped through to a well-worn page. The first time she'd seen this book, she had little hope it offered the right type of amusement for one of her elegant affairs. But now she knew it held all the answers.

*****

Nine days later, Harriet welcomed a dozen guests into her parlour. Alice arrived last, making a fuss and attracting much attention, but

Harriet did not let it affect her. Nothing would quiet her spirits this night.

The sophisticated crowd mingled and nibbled at the buffet supper, served on her Doulton plates with the cobalt blue Persian spray, the aristocratic tinkle of her Roger Brothers silverware on porcelain filling the room. Harriet could see how impressed everyone was. Even Alice failed to find fault with her service. Harriet quivered with pleasure.

Once the guests were sated, Harriet signalled her husband to make a toast to the hostess, which she had scripted and they had rehearsed. Harriet, naturally, blushed at the praise.

Then, it was time to introduce the amusements.

"Ladies and gentlemen," Harriet said, "this evening I have a series of most sensational entertainments for your pleasure. Inspired by a book of children's amusements, I have transformed some games, developed them into mature recreations, guaranteed to titillate and tantalize a modern crowd. This will not be an evening for the fainthearted!"

There were murmurs of approval and a smattering of applause. A pair of widowed sisters who wintered abroad tittered nervously.

"I'm sure you've heard of parties where guests partake of a gaseous inebriant."

"Nitrous oxide," said Alice. She sat in a carved rosewood bergère, looking down her nose, as if she were queen on the throne. "I've been to those parties. Very exclusive affairs."

"Of course, you have, dear," said Harriet. "Which is why you will be the first to take the gas." She smiled at a suddenly red-faced Alice.

"You procured laughing gas?" said a senior partner from her husband's firm. "How jolly!"

"I have not procured it. I have made it! From instructions in the children's book, if you can imagine."

"But is it safe?" asked a spinster with a dull countenance and a fine inheritance.

"It has been tested most thoroughly and is of highest quality. And what could be safer than a child's amusement?" Harriet rang a bell. The butler brought in a bulging bag made of oiled silk with a small stoppered tube sewn into its mouth. "Of course," she continued, "those who do not wish to take part in my modern games may retire to the library to play cards."

No one moved.

Harriet gestured towards Alice, and the butler presented her with the silk bag.

"H-how delightful," said Alice. "But I have tried this gas before. I shall go last, so that all may have a fair turn."

"Not to worry, dear Alice. There is plenty of gas. Oodles of it. You go ahead."

All eyes were on Alice, which emboldened her exhibitionist spirit. She brought the tube up to her mouth, then hesitated. The butler did not. He pulled the stopper, pinched Alice's nose shut and simultaneously squeezed the bag, forcing a cloud of gas into Alice's gaping mouth. Alice sputtered, tried to pull back, but within seconds the gas had taken effect. She sagged back into her chair, giggling and wriggling her fingers in time to music only she could hear.

Soon, guests were dancing and singing and twirling with glee. Harriet, ever the gracious hostess, circulated soberly among them, making sure all were merry and no impropriety was observed. She noticed that Alice was flushed and sent her to the dressing room to apply pearl white powder to her ruddy complexion. She complimented several others on their dancing skills.

After thirty minutes, when the euphoric effects of the gas had gentled but not dissipated, Harriet announced it was time for a game. The guests hurrahed.

"When I first inhaled the gas," Harriet told them, "I felt the warm embrace of the spirit world. I have invited those spirits to join us in our games tonight."

"Ooh wee woo," a woman with extravagant pearls sang to a potted plant. "Let the spirits come!"

"Indeed!" Harriet assembled her guests in a circle and bade them hold hands. "The spirits have sent a message. The first to divine it will be the winner."

At this cue, the butler extinguished the lights. Yelps and nervous laughter greeted the darkness. They continued to hold hands, trying—and failing—to maintain a somber regard, until a well-to-do banker shouted, "Look! There, above the fireplace."

Everyone turned and saw illuminated writing on the wall.

Beware the black devil amongst you.

"My goodness!" Harriet chuckled. "That is not the message I expected. Though, I must say, beware to any devil that attempts to ruin my party!"

The guests hooted and showed their support. The lights returned and servants circulated with inflated bags. The banker, as the winner, received the first bag. The other guests pushed and shoved and impatiently grabbed at the remaining bags. The befuddled guests were soon draped across the stylish couches, snickering and snorting and yelping with pleasure.

Harriet let them have a brief rest before calling out the next game.

"Not only are there spirits here with us, but there are magic spiders, too," she said. "Otherworldly fiends, made of trickery and turpitude. Find them, kill them, before their wickedness can spread. The most kills wins."

The guests whooped and staggered around the room, flipping cushions and shaking curtains. A spider was found by the pianoforte and, when smashed underfoot, gave off a loud bang. The room echoed with guffaws.

"Bravo!" Harriet shouted as she circled behind the chairs. "Look everywhere."

"Aagh." Alice laughed. "They are upon me." She slapped playfully at the creatures made of cloth and fulminating silver that Harriet had tossed in her lap and around her seat, squealing as each one popped loudly.

"So much evil here," Harriet said, standing behind Alice, and giving her a sharp pinch that made her scream.

The shriek, coupled with the explosions, sent the intoxicated guests into a frenzy. They swarmed, beating at spiders, pounding upon Alice herself in their excitement. "Aagh!" Alice shouted in pain and bewilderment. "Stop."

Harriet waited another minute before declaring Alice the winner. She handed a bruised and horrified Alice the gas, which she accepted with shaking hands. Within minutes Alice forgot all about the spider-hunters.

Servants passed around more gas. A few quick breaths and the debauchees collapsed about the room, each enjoying a euphoria of their own imagination.

But Harriet would not let them rest long. She had games to play.

"Well done, my darlings. You have vanquished the spiders. What say we carry on?"

A dozen voices slurred together in varying degrees of affirmation. Some tried to get up. Most lacked the facility to coordinate bodily movement.

"Stay where you are." Harriet reassured them. "I have a bottle of Harrogate water. We will pass it around and whomever can identify the exact nature of the water's particular scent will be the winner."

The butler passed the bottle under the nose of each guest. The foul odour provoked many awkward contortions and hilarious reactions. Guesses rang out, each more creative and depraved than the next.

Alice was last. The butler held the bottle under her nose. The sulphuretted hydrogen fumes rose up and interacted with the pearl white. In mere seconds, Alice's pale face had turned the colour of pitch.

"My god!" A woman in an expensive French gown pointed at Alice. "She has turned black."

"Black as a devil," said Harriet.

"She IS the black devil!" shouted a second cousin to a viscount.

Alice looked around. "Who?"

"You, Alice. You are a devil, and now everyone sees it. Did you think I would not know it was you who cursed me and threatened me with catastrophe?"

"I don't understand," said a befuddled Alice. "Why would I do such things? We're the dearest of friends."

"I'll admit you had me fooled. But the spirits knew better."

Alice struggled to rise from her chair, but Harriet pushed her back and held her down.

"Time for the last game of the night, my laughing friends. The spirits have shown us a true devil. Like with the treacherous spiders, we must destroy this evil. Any who strike a blow for righteousness will get a great blessing and be delivered from all calamity."

A tremendous clamour followed. Too intoxicated to know rhyme from reason, the guests acted impulsively and violently, not for the first time that evening. They stumbled about, grabbing whatever weapons they could find as they moved towards Alice. Her eyes bulged, fear fraying the edge of her dreamy drug haze, making her appear even more diabolical. The mob cried out for blood. Alice screamed as the unhinged revelers descended upon her.

Harriet turned away and Cora handed her a green silk bag. Harriet inhaled deeply as she relaxed into a blue velvet couch. She sighed with satisfaction as the spirits appeared before her once more, luminous wisps that held secret knowledge, keepers of pleasure for which language has no name, her most faithful and dearest friends.

"We told you," they said in their ethereal voices. "This party will make all the papers."

Ozymandias

Thomas Farr

Reality TV Star | A Comet

She studied the city off in the distance. The juts of towers and high-rises like broken teeth biting into the blackened flesh of night. The thick fog layer that coated the buildings and streets with a phlegm-coloured film, heavy as spores on the hot August air. A cold polyp of moon moved through a shattered brocade of cloud. She looked for stars but found none. Found nothing save the dished reflection of the city's restive lights.

She sat on the bonnet of the car for a while and smoked a cigarette and thought about things. She sighed as she exhaled, studying the thin blue patterns the smoke made as though perhaps they'd tell her what a midnight drive into the hills hadn't.

Her phone vibrated beside her. She glanced at the screen, unlocked it and typed out a quick reply, then spun her cigarette butt off into the darkness and slid down from the bonnet and got back into the car and drove on.

It was past two a.m. by the time she arrived at Erin's place. She checked her face in the mirror, hid her tired eyes behind a pair of sunglasses and scanned the street for paparazzi. Bass music throbbed like a bad hangover. The naked skull of moon shivered with fierce metallic lustre; its crater-mottled coinage a face in profile that seemed to turn towards her. Then she was out of the car and into the party, pasted by a strobe of sickly crimson light in which everything seemed to move faster and faster, her surroundings changing moment by moment, faces sloshing past in alcohol-fuelled carousel and the air threaded with a heady mingled reek of sweat and marijuana. Abruptly the ceiling peeled away and she found herself standing beneath open sky, her eyes lost in a study of translucent clouds with pinpricks of light shining through.

'Jess.'

She turned towards the voice. Vampy red dress, hair piled high, green eyes shining out of a pale mask of face. A martini in one hand and a smouldering joint in the other.

Erin pressed the fresh drink into her hand. 'Not yet,' she said, gazing up at the clouds, the sky. Jessica slugged the cocktail and steadied herself on the edge of the roof.

'Not yet what?'

'Ozymandias.'

The syllables swirled through the great dark cave of Jessica's head. *Ozymandias.* The comet that had been all over the news and socials lately.

Erin dragged hard on the joint and exhaled. When she spoke, her voice was thick and blurred from the smoke, and didn't sound like Erin at all. 'Look on my works, ye mighty, and despair. Ha! But listen. Darling. I heard about the show.'

Down went the dregs of the drink. She leaned her forearms on the wall and dangled the empty glass by its stem.

'Fuck it,' she said. 'I'm doing dinner with Arquette tomorrow. He might pick it up.' *If he's clawed his way back from the brink of bankruptcy.*

'I don't get it.' Erin moved up beside her. Smoke curled from the joint and the scent of it constricted the air; she handed it to Jessica, who drew deeply, exhaled and handed it back. 'Milo was absolutely gushing about you when I bumped into him at The Frolic last month.'

'Of course he was. I was still fucking him then.'

Silence span a heavy web. It snared bass throb, traffic sounds and jagged shrieks of laughter. When Jessica next spoke, it snapped.

'I'm sick of it. Arseholes like him. We shouldn't be forced to give ourselves up to get somewhere.'

'We shouldn't.' The clouds parted and the moon's bright clean face hove up through them. 'But needs must. Ozymandias passes next week. There'll be a party. Milo's invited. We both know he'll come.'

Erin's hand brushed her forearm. The glass slipped from her fingers and fell like a dream between her and the ground and shattered into stars on the tiles far below.

'Be there when he does.'

***

'Damn it.' Arquette snapped his fingers to call the waiter back. 'Get some vermouth in this and shake it properly next time.'

He turned back to Jessica and showed his teeth. 'The service in here is fucking atrocious nowadays.'

She smiled and picked at the salad he'd ordered for her. Outside on the street lurked a man with a camera welded to his eye. *Snap. Snap, snap snap.* She tried to ignore him as headlines tickertaped through her mind: *DON'T SWIPE RIGHT* STAR PUCKERS UP TO DELACOY JR . . . IS DISGRACED *MALFUNCTIONS* DIRECTOR JESSICA JAUDEN'S LATEST VICTIM? And so on, et cetera, et cetera.

Once they'd finished eating Arquette fumbled around for his wallet; Jessica tapped plastic for both meals and drinks—now *that* was a hit, dinner for two at La Sacré Cœur—and let him lead her out to the car. The evening and late summer light danced on chrome and glass. He'd been drinking but insisted on driving. Up, up, up into the hills, up past fan palms tall as giraffes, meadow slopes of chaparral and scrub. Finally he parked lee of a radio tower and killed the engine. In the red dusk the hills about seemed like hills transposed from some alien landscape; the endless dunes of Mars bloodied by the light of oxide moons. The windows were down and cool fingers of breeze reached in. A coyote howled down the last reaches of day, long and plaintive as anything that ever was.

Then Arquette's hand was chasing her thigh and he was kissing her hard, working his tongue into her mouth, reek of cheap cologne and martini breath rolling over her in sick miasmic waves.

We shouldn't. But needs must. The words skulked through her mind like a black cat down a midnight alley. She just needed to disconnect. Go someplace else. Descend to that dark mirror realm where the things that happened happened to another her, another Jessica who was empty, vacuous of all self. It would be easy to—

Without knowing she was going to she shoved him off, hard, harder still when he struggled against her.

'What the *fuck?*' He leaned back into the driver's seat and looked at her the way someone might look at something distasteful stuck to the bottom of their shoe.

'I don't want it,' she said. She was fumbling for the door handle and then she was out, out into the cooling Californian air, the steady buzz of insects and the hills going opaque with night. Arquette shouted that she was a bitch, a whore, that nobody would ever pick up her *stupid fucking show.* She turned to face the car. Erin grinned from the backseat, made a shushing gesture with one long, needle-like finger. Her teeth shone, sheathed by her lips; her face was hard and bone-white, like glazed and fire porcelain. Before Jessica could speak, Arquette leaned over and yanked the passenger's door shut. 'Cunt.' He slewed the car into reverse and turned and hightailed it out of the radio tower's shadow. Dust settled slowly through sudden silence. She stood and watched as the car's red brakelights vaulted away into darkness. 'Well fuck,' she said at last, and began to walk.

***

She lay awake well into the small hours of the morning. Doomscrolling past famine and war, murder, rape, natural disaster. And Ozymandias. Always, on every platform, every news channel. RARE GLACIAL COMET TO PASS BY EARTH FOR FIRST TIME IN 75,000 YEARS. An Italian astrologist talking about psychic debris and the 'lens of the Zodiac'. Eggheads from NASA arguing over flight paths and trajectories. A presidential forerunner calling it an omen, a sign. She swiped out of her news feed and pulled up Erin's contact. Swiped it away. Pulled it back. Swiped it away.

'Fuck.' She didn't understand any of it. And just below the thin veneer of confusion and unease: the creeping, gnawing knowledge that *Don't Swipe Right* was dead in the water. And then what? Become reality TV's latest well-documented car crash? The paparazzi would have a field day with her. *As if they don't already.* She supposed there was always the east coast or Canada. A fresh start. A clean break. She got up and made her way across the cold tiled floor to the balcony. The moon was full and sloshed with shadow. Dogs barked. A siren blurt-blurted. Somewhere a woman screamed, a frisson of fear or excitement or both in nigh indistinguishable blend. She thought about Milo then. Everything he'd promised her. Everything he'd done to her and made her do. Her fingers tightened on the balcony railing. *There'll be a party. Be there.*

***

Dance music unspooled through strobic rooms. The night was a record and Jessica the needle spiralling down its endless groove. She couldn't remember what she'd taken. Decided it didn't matter, nothing mattered; not Milo, not *Don't Swipe Right* and certainly not the fucking comet everyone was up on the roof staring at. She was a star going supernova, skirting the edge of a black hole. And maybe that was okay. Maybe blackness wasn't so bad after all.

The void yearned.

Someone handed her a tall tequila tonic and led her to a huge open-plan living room with a fireplace that might have come from a castle. A producer she knew but whose name she couldn't recall smooched with doe-eyed starlets. The room twitched. Someone else kissed bruises on her neck in the kitchen, the edge of the granite worktop pressing uncomfortably into the small of her back. Then the man stiffened and stood very still with an expression almost of speculation, as if he'd decoded some secret and was deciding whether or not to reveal it. Something emerged palely into his eyes like a face condensing in a window at night. He slipped away and fell, his features already drained of colour; a blanched white flower floating in the pool of blood in which it had fallen.

'Hey. Hey, hey, it's okay.' She was being led away now, out of the kitchen and along a hallway that was alternately lightless and not, pulsing diastoles of ceiling light spilling a scarlet glow. A man with bleached hair swept back from a high forehead and a warlord's weight of chunky gold chains slumped against the wall. He had one hand pressed to his throat and was shivering as if immersed in icy water.

The red light seeped away to silver; moonlight so acute that everything seemed carved in bas-relief. Her vision wheeled. A thousand houses spun below her. Slowly, slowly she straightened up. The cool air was clearing her head. The stars still trembled and the moon still shuddered, but now she could see why. A violent sheer of light down the sky to the south; a bismuth flood of phosphorescence like a rip in the fabric of space itself through which shone colours of an unknown spectrum, the sickly hues of long-rotted stars in some other cosmology than this.

Milo's face glistened where he knelt. Erin's was a glazed clay mask. There were other women and other men. The men knelt, bound and sobbing. The women cavorted. Strange daubings slathered their bare chests and faces. Erin slipped the straps of Jessica's dress over her shoulders and let it fall. Her hands were thick with dark red wetness, her palm smearing Jessica's chest, her throat, the underside of her chin. Her nostrils flared with stenches of iron and fear; she thought she caught a hint of cheap cologne, a ghost of martini breath and La Sacré Cœur.

Cutlery flashed. A symphony of kitchen knives and carving forks. Her blood bespoke a slow hypnotic chant. A hymn. An invitation.

We shouldn't. But needs must.

She seized Milo's gaze. His eyes were all pupil, ink-black pools in which her own marbled apparition grew and grew and grew as she crossed the rooftop.

She hunkered down beside him and smiled.

Overhead, Ozymandias flared.

Money, Beauty, and Brains

Linda M. Bayley

A Confidence Trickster | A Diary

Dear Diary,

Today was Travis's funeral. It was closed casket, of course.

***

Morning is always quiet at the Breaking Bread Food Bank. That's when we stack the donations up in the warehouse out back, put hampers together, get receipts sent out. I mean, they don't let me handle the money. But I know that's what they do in the back office. I hear them talking about it on breaks sometimes. So-and-so donated this much, what's-her-name donated so much more. That lady we saw on TV the other night? You wouldn't *believe* how much she sent in!

I don't mind working here. I think I might volunteer here even if I weren't doing community service. The work keeps my hands busy while my mind focuses on my next job. There's always a next job to think about.

And then there she is, walking through the front door, looking to volunteer. Older than I'd like, maybe fiftyish, but a nice pink business suit, blonde hair, and curves in all the right places. The lady from the TV. The rich one.

***

Dear Diary,

It's time I stopped wallowing. Travis wouldn't want this for me. So I went down to the Breaking Bread Food Bank, where Melinda always volunteers, and asked if I could have a couple of shifts in between surgeries. They were surprised to see me, of course, but it's good to set an example. I start Saturday.

***

Today I'm training the new volunteer. Valerie is her name. I show her the warehouse, and all the canned soup stocked up on the shelves. "The thing about canned soup," I tell her, "is that everybody donates it, but most of the cans don't have pull tabs. People never think about the can openers. That's the first thing you learn when you start here."

"Can openers, check." She pulls a notebook out of the pocket of her jeans and makes a little note like she's hanging on my every word.

When we take a break for coffee she tells me she's a brain surgeon. Which is interesting, I guess. More importantly, she's a widow.

***

Dear Diary,

I met a man at the food bank today who looks just like Travis. Same build, same height. His name is Shane. I think he might be the perfect candidate. Best part? He's an ex-con. Nobody's going to miss him.

***

I'm getting ready to ask Valerie out when *she* asks *me*. "I can get to know you a lot better away from this warehouse," she tells me.

She picks me up in her Porsche and we go to this bar I've never been to before. One of her favourite bands is playing later, and she can't wait to introduce me to their sound. I'm imagining folk songs and fiddles, but it's this hard rock band with flannel shirts and surf-dyed hair. They launch into Nirvana's *Aneurysm* and Valerie flies to the dance floor, letting her hair down and thrashing around like a cheerleader on speed. I'm too astonished to join in.

"So… you like Nirvana?" I ask as she sits down, breathless.

She laughs and takes a swig of my beer, then starts to peel away the Molson's label. "My dear boy," she says in a grandmother voice. "Just how old do you think I am? And how old were *you* when Kurt Cobain died?"

I signal the server for another Canadian, since Valerie shows no signs of giving mine back. Truth be told, I can't remember when Kurt Cobain died. But my date doesn't need to know that.

***

Dear Diary,

A young body like Shane's is absolutely wasted on such an immature mind. But we'll get that sorted out, soon enough.

***

Valerie and I are getting along well, but I don't think she trusts me enough to bring her back to her place yet. She's probably counting the silverware while she gets ready for me to visit. Like it's her *silver* I'm after.

She's come to my place a couple of times. I don't have much, just a bachelor apartment with a fold-out couch, but she doesn't seem to mind. And she's wild in bed. I had no idea someone so old would have so much energy. I shouldn't kiss and tell. Except to say this: she likes what I've got, too. After the first time, we were lying on my lumpy couch, sweaty and breathless, and she was practically purring as she drew her finger up and down my chest and belly.

"Yes, you'll do," she whispered, though it sounded like it was more to herself than to me. "You'll do very nicely."

It will almost break my heart to break hers. Almost.

***

Dear Diary,

I think it's time to bring my boy toy home and turn him into a man.

Finally, Valerie brings me to her place. She has to pick me up again, because the city bus doesn't go out to her neighbourhood. I've never been out this way before, and the only word I can think of to describe the houses is "palatial." They seem bigger and fancier than mansions. If this is the kind of life a brain surgeon's salary can buy, maybe I should have stayed in school a little longer.

We're kissing by the time we get to her front door. She pushes me inside, all hot and ready, then says, "I want to show you something." She takes me by the hand and leads me down a set of stairs hidden behind a narrow door in the living room wall.

At the bottom is a white-tiled room, brightly lit, with a bed in the middle. The bed has four sets of handcuffs dangling from it.

"What is this, some kind of sex dungeon?" I ask.

She smiles, wickedly. "Something like that." She starts to unbutton her blouse and says, "Take off your shirt and get on the bed."

I like a woman who knows what she wants. I peel off my tee and lie down. Slowly, sensually, she cuffs my hands and feet to the bed.

"What's the safe word?" I ask.

"There is no safety here, Shane." She shucks her blouse and puts on a white lab coat.

"Are we playing Doctor?" I joke.

She doesn't smile. "Just try to relax." She leaves the room through a door I hadn't noticed and comes back with… Is that a brain in a jar?

"You haven't met my husband, but he's been looking forward to meeting you!"

"What the hell?"

"He can't hear you or see you, of course, but he's perfectly conscious. All thanks to a nutrient bath I developed in medical school." She sets the jar down on a table beside the bed and gazes fondly at the brain. "He's been very patient, waiting for me to find the perfect new body for him to live in. And it's not like you're doing anything useful with yours, except trying to romance older women for their money."

I must be losing my touch, if she saw through me. I struggle against the handcuffs, but they hold tight.

She pulls a bone saw from somewhere under the bed and says, "I'm afraid this will hurt. A lot."

"Wait," I say, "wait, just let me go, and we'll call it even. I won't tell anyone I was ever here." Sweat's pooling in my eyes, or is it tears?

"Sorry, not sorry, but you're not going anywhere until after I'm done with you." She plugs in the bone saw and turns on its whirring blade.

"At least knock me out!" I plead. I feel a sudden warmth in my groin as my bladder lets go. A distant part of me wonders if my bowels will go next.

"If I anesthetize you, the drugs will damage the brain as it settles into its new host. I can't risk harming my Travis."

She tilts the bone saw towards my face. My hands try to jerk up, to cover my face, to save me from what's coming. The metal cuffs bite into the skin of my wrists. The bone saw cuts into my skull and I scream, sobbing as blood floods into my eyes.

I would pray, but right now I can't even remember the name of God.

***

Dear Diary,

Bermuda is beautiful this time of year. Travis and I always wanted to come here, but we had so little time together before the cancer took his body. But now, on our second honeymoon, it feels like we have all the time in the world. The scar on his forehead is healing nicely, and when people ask him if he was one of my patients he just laughs and tells them he was in a bar fight.

As for Shane, he ditched on the last of his community service hours at the Breaking Bread Food Bank and skipped town. Nobody's seen him since. I doubt they're even looking.

***

I think. I exist. Or I'm dead. I don't know. I might just be a brain in a jar. I have no mouth to scream, no eyes to see, no skin to feel the breeze, no hands to keep busy while I think about my next job.

My next job. There is no next job, no home to go back to, no life to look forward to.

There is only this. And a dream of revenge.

The Last Picture

Ash Egan

Conservationist | Photo Album

As the Archivist, it was my job to document everything. The abundance and beauty of the forest. The annual cycle of wither and bloom. Each week I would take my pictures and add them to the album, just as my predecessors did. I did not expect to be the one who would document the end.

That day, I arrived early. I stumbled down the steep slope, beneath the canopy of trees and into the wild valley. The sun was just cresting the horizon and the leaves dripped with morning dew.

Just outside the treeline were the chainsaws and bulldozers and wood chippers. They lay dormant, waiting to growl into action. Poised to devour.

I was thankful that my companions had not yet arrived to start their preparations. Thankful for some final moments of peace with this place, before the machines came to flatten it. To extinguish all life.

I reached the clearing where we would always meet to lay our hedges or pull up weeds. Our plastic tool shed was there, locked up tight, chains wrapped around the handles in a bunch. In the centre, a lone camp chair stood empty. Just as our ritual dictates, it sat a constant vigil before Old Redferne.

The thousand-year-old oak tree towered above the rest. Moss and sprouting fungus decorated its bark and glittered in the early light of the autumn morning. Even now, it fizzed and hummed in anticipation.

I raised my Instax camera and snapped a picture.

I knelt closer to the roots, where they formed an archway as they split into the ground. Mounds of mushrooms clustered in the hollow, Amethyst Deceivers and Chicken of the Woods. Dead Man's Fingers clawed their way out of the soil.

Underneath the ground, they all weaved together. The roots formed pathways that connected and embraced each other. Shared knowledge and memories.

It's this idea that drew me to The Society. Like me, each member had lost something or someone. They coaxed me out into nature during my darkest moments. My loss was eased by the connection and submission to something older than myself. By this community of the damaged looking for peace and purpose in the forest. Nature offers no answers, but asks fewer questions.

I snapped another picture. One that may be the last of this place.

The Conservationist arrived. The sound of slick mud and breaking branches alerted me to his presence. He was the leader of The Society and had been for longer than I'd been alive. There are many photos of him in the album.

"I thought I'd be the first," he said.

"I wanted to capture every moment. Before it's taken from us." I said.

He placed his hand on my shoulder. "You'll be taking pictures of Old Redferne long after I'm gone. She has seen ages of men come and go."

The ground around the tree thrummed in affirmation.

Then the diesel engines spluttered into life beyond the treeline. Men laughed and joked at the edge of the forest. Petrol fumes and smoke diffused into the air.

"It's starting." The Conservationist unlocked the chain from the shed door. He carried it over to Old Redferne and began to wrap it around the trunk in loops. Shafts of light filtered through the leaves as the sun rose above the canopy.

I went into the shed to get the photo album so I could add pictures as I took them. Not knowing when or if I'd get the chance later. The leather-bound volume sat in a half-shattered plastic tub.

Scuffed and smeared with dirt. On the front, it said *Moments to remember*. Like an old manor house, it creaked open to reveal its ghosts. The pages were wrinkled and stained with water damage and had to be peeled apart.

I flicked past those first sepia photos of The Society's founders. Four women in straw sun hats and frilled dresses that reached from ear to ankle. They leant on shovels and rakes and smiled in front of Old Redferne. The inscription read: *Clearing the way - the first meeting of the Hulsted Conservationists*. Turning the page passed a decade or more. The women were gone and a small cairn had been piled in front of the tree.

At the edge of the woods, rubber tracks rolled over branches and bushes. They crackled like a campfire as they were crushed underneath.

The Horticulturist arrived next. She edged down the hill led by her grandson, The Apprentice. She held her stick in one hand and his arm in the other. White hair sprouted from beneath her threadbare cap and her limbs were thin as kindling inside her all-weather gear.

"The Artisans are right behind us," she said, her voice wavering. "They have The Offering."

Down in the clearing, she unhooked her arm from The Apprentice and knelt to cradle the wisps of a Ghost Orchid in her hand.

"It's a rare flower that blooms in such adversity."

I snapped another picture as a tear rolled down her cheek.

In the album, I had reached Edwardian moustaches and flat caps. The Horticulturist herself is in that picture, at her first meeting. A baby leaning against a moss-covered cairn. She stares into the camera as her mother and father embrace in front of Old Redferne. On the next page, a generation has come and gone and she is old enough to wield a scythe. Two more cairns lie in front of the tree. Old Redferne stands unchanged.

The machines rose into a cacophony of idling engines and choking exhausts. The workers waded through the brush towards us.

Ahead of them were The Artisans, who arrived carrying a huge wooden footlocker. They shuffled down the muddy slope carrying it between them, one holding up the back while the other braced the front on his shoulders. When they reached level ground, the oblong box swung nearly out of their hands and the contents rolled and thumped inside. The Artisans were strong, but even they struggled with the weight of The Offering.

They set it down in the middle of the clearing, in front of Old Redferne, and left the key resting on top. It shook and rocked on its edges, the padlock knocking against the side. The Artisans stepped back and to the side, never taking their eyes off their cargo, as though it was a bomb set to explode.

The Conservationist moved around behind it. From inside, muffled cries and thuds. Hands and feet hammering against the wood.

Behind us, above the ridge, engines revved and motors cranked.

"Thank you all for coming," The Conservationist used the box like an altar, his arms spread wide. "Today, those men have come to take a tree that's stood for millennia. An organism that contains multitudes. The hub of a singular ecosystem. A whole world, which they plan to eradicate. A tree that we and our forebears have protected for more than a hundred years."

The Horticulturist nodded and closed her eyes. The Apprentice, a young man and a new member of The Society, watched the box closely, the cogs in his mind turning. The Artisans stood motionless, hands behind their backs, watching Old Redferne. I raised my camera.

"We may be few, but our strength lives in our conviction and our sacrifice. Our unshakeable commitment to protect our home." He picked up the key and turned it in the rusty padlock. "Our commitment to do what has to be done to protect this place as our forebears did before us."

In one motion he lifted the lid and upended the box in front of us. A cluster of limbs and damp hair flopped out into the mud and The Horticulturist smothered a gasp with her withered hand.

The Offering was tied at the wrists and ankles. She writhed and moaned in the dirt, trying to stand.

The Apprentice stumbled backwards, tripping over the chair. Horror clamped his mouth and eyes open. The Offering rose to all fours and swung her hair back, fixing us with a desperate, wide-eyed glare.

She had green eyes. What was visible of her face was tacky with dark blood and wet mud. She grunted and pleaded from behind a grimy cloth gag.

She tried to stand and run but the slick surface gave way beneath her and she thudded to the ground.

The engines were not far away now. The laughter and rasping of the chainsaws drew closer.

The Artisans moved forward and grasped The Offering under her arms, lifting her off her feet. She struggled but they were too strong. When she looked into their faces and saw their expressions of serene pity, the rage died in her eyes. It dissolved into hopeless anguish and bitter tears as they carried her back around behind the box and towards the tree, towards the chains.

The Conservationist moved aside as they sat her at the base of the tree, on top of the fronds of fungus that grasped around her thighs. She tried to curl away from them, into the foetal position but they held her legs. They fixed her to Old Redferne with the chains, bridging the gap where it split into the thick roots that burrowed into the soil.

The Conservationist knelt before her, before Old Redferne, as they held her and wound the chains.

The ground was vibrating. It could have been the advance of the machines or the struggle but it felt like something in the tree was waking up.

"Mother of the forest." The Conservationist raised his voice and his hands in exultation. "Accept this offering. Accept this sacrifice."

I held my camera in front of my eyes. The dirt shook beneath our feet.

Afraid to watch but unable to look away, I gazed unblinking through the viewfinder. I was lucky. As The Archivist, the camera offered me a separation. A barrier the others didn't have. Insulation from reality.

That's why, even though I'd been told what to expect, it still felt like a movie when the archway convulsed and contracted. When the roots separated and birthed slick, black claws. Knuckled fingers and spindly limbs that curved around The Offering. Slid over her neck, breasts and thighs. They grasped and scratched at her, smearing her skin with oozing black resin. Pulling her screaming into the bark, her teeth gnashing over the gag in her mouth.

She tried to wedge herself in the gap but it was too late.

My finger hovered over the button as she began to fold into the hollow beneath Old Redferne. I saw the whites of her eyes as she comprehended her fate and the tree cradled her in response.

The crashing and sawing and churning of the engines advanced close enough to drown out even her muffled cries, The Apprentice's sobbing and even the soft singing of The Horticulturist as she rocked back and forth at my side.

My finger rested on the button until the arms pulled her back into the tree, devouring her. A leg, with ripped black jeans and one bare foot, spasmed and strained, engulfed in bark and fungus.

The Conservationist dropped prone and began to stack small stones on top of each other on the turf. When he was finished, he slithered away like a serpent.

I held off, as I'd been told, until the roots and the bark and the mushrooms closed the ground over her foot. Until she had been swallowed whole.

Then, *Click*.

The cacophony of screams and cries and engines and chainsaws and chattering and laughter all stopped.

The forest was still. The only sound was the whir of the camera ejecting the new picture.

I pulled it out and held it up to my face, watching as it developed. Watching the image of a thousand-year-old oak tree and a little stone cairn emerge from the formless white void.

Perhaps not the last picture after all.

The Final Course

Heather Scott

Petrologist | Twelve-Course Dinner

Jonas raises a pastry fork and taps it against his champagne glass. Tradition in his family states that whenever somebody gets engaged, they all come together to celebrate with a twelve-course meal. During the final course—and not before—the couple shares the story of their engagement. Jonas winks over at Caroline, who is clutching a viridian stone in her left hand. It glistens like a diamond in the light. His grandmother, Ingrid, watches with an adoring smile, while the rest of the table prepares to silence their chatter. Jonas begins with a smirk. "I know you've been waiting for this all night, so here's the truth. This proposal story begins... with a troll."

The guests erupt in laughter, including Jonas. Caroline absent-mindedly rubs the stone, as Ingrid's smile slowly fades. Once the chuckling subsides, Jonas reminds everyone of the stories the family matriarch regaled them with in childhood. Stories of the trolls that live deep in the Norwegian mountains, and how they hunt at night because the sunlight will turn them to stone. "To my American fiancé, I'm sure this sounds absurd," Jonas proceeds. "But by the end of this story, you're going to realize what an incredible man you're marrying." Ignoring the eye rolls around the table, he continues on.

While visiting his grandmother in Norway, Jonas had spent weeks in the mountains trying to collect rock samples that he could fashion into a one-of-a-kind gift for Caroline. One of his petrology colleagues had had luck finding eclogite in the area—a rare stone often referred to as "Christmas rock" for its distinctive red and green coloring. Jonas knew a stone like that would be perfect for Caroline, but so far his efforts had not been fortuitous.

Deep in the woods one afternoon, considering a contingency plan, Jonas spotted a field of moss near a large spruce. Upon closer inspection the terrain gave way, plunging Jonas underground. He managed to grab onto a tree root to keep himself from plummeting to the dirt. Initially scrabbling to get back up, Jonas stilled when he heard grunting and scratching from beneath him. Looking down he spied the opening to a large cave, and curiosity got the best of him. Grabbing a granola bar from his backpack, he dropped it to the ground, then pulled himself up with the root, positioning his body so he could see below. And that's when a monstrously large, humanoid hand reached out and snatched the granola bar. Jonas hung from the root in stunned silence for a moment, and then he clambered to the surface, and he ran.

Jonas' mind raced as he thought about the lore he had grown up listening to and compared it to what he had seen. A hand, at least twice as big as his own, with grotesquely long fingernails, and skin the lifeless color of a corpse. He considered how easy it was to lure the being out of hiding, and remembered what he had learned as a child—trolls turn to stone in the sunlight. Stone. He devised a plan.

A granola bar may have worked once, but if the legends were true, Jonas knew that what a troll really craved was meat. He spent the next morning setting traps to catch anything he could. Guilt gnawed at him initially, but his desire to do something exceptional for Caroline, to prove his love, triumphed in the end. By noon the only fatalities were a red squirrel and a hare, but they would have to do. Jonas traced his steps back to the spruce, and with a deep breath he tossed the hare down in front of the cave opening. He grabbed a rope from his pack and tied it around the squirrel's waist. Soon, the grunting he had heard just a day earlier reappeared. When the troll emerged this time, Jonas was able to see it in its entirety. Even stooped over he could tell it was immense, the skin on its bulbous nose dry and cracked as it sniffed the air. It picked up the hare in one meaty palm, tossing it in its gargantuan mouth and swallowing it whole. Shaking, Jonas used the rope he was holding to lower the squirrel down the wall toward the cave. Sliding his body as far away from the opening in the ground as he could, he held onto the rope and waited. The tug on the other end was so forceful that it dragged him forward, and Jonas had to release the rope to avoid being pulled to his death. Jonas hung terrified over the edge of the opening, realizing the troll had not only spotted him, but had devoured the squirrel and intended to ravage him next. It dug its fingernails into the dirt, eyes trained on its next meal, as Jonas scrambled to right himself.

Heart pounding, Jonas scurried to his feet and looked frantically at his surroundings. The large spruce at the surface of the hole meant that the sunlight he had hoped for was stifled. He looked behind him to see the troll—at least eight feet tall—rising to its feet. Jonas took off running, but he could feel the earth shaking as the giant gave chase. Knowing that his only hope was to make it to an open space, Jonas silently prayed as he pumped his legs faster than he thought possible. Seeing sunlight up ahead, he used one final burst of energy to propel him into a clearing, tripping on a half-buried rock in the process. Tears rushing down his face, he turned to see the troll approaching at full speed. Jonas put his forearms up in a protective posture and covered his face, but as the troll reached the clearing—and the sunlight—it froze instantly in a lunging position. His face inches from its petrified hand, Jonas laid his head back on the earth and sobbed.

He pauses at this point in the story to take in the reactions of his family members. Each of them fully engrossed in what Jonas imagines is the greatest engagement tale they've ever heard. All except Ingrid, who is looking down at her plate, wringing her napkin between her hands.

The stone troll was more magnificent than Jonas could have imagined. Colors from oyster to onyx were marbled throughout, and in the light were glints of green - small flecks like emerald sprinkled amid the rock. Jonas grabbed his bag of tools and began the arduous process of chipping away at the form, a labor of love. Upon reaching the center of the troll's chest he discovered a small stone that was such a vibrant shade of green it took his breath away. He knew then that this would be how he'd propose to Caroline—a stolen heart for the woman who'd stolen his.

As if on cue, Caroline holds the green heart up toward the light for the other guests to see. "We're going to turn it into jewelry, but I haven't decided what yet," she beams. Jonas' family members, all of whom had made special trips here for this occasion, begin to rise from the table to get a closer look at the stone.

"That is breathtaking…" gushes a cousin.

"Did you take any photos?" inquires another.

The chatter grows louder, when Ingrid stands vehemently from her chair, smashing her champagne glass in the process.

"Shut up, you fools!" she howls. "Have you no idea what Jonas has done? Did my stories teach you nothing?!"

Jonas stands from his chair, his arms out in surrender, as the rest of the guests cautiously begin to sit. "Whoa, Gram," Jonas says gently. "Calm down. What are you trying to say?"

"These creatures," she begins, "are not to be trifled with. I used to tell you those stories because I hoped they would scare you away from looking for trouble." Jonas and Caroline lock eyes across the table, shift uncomfortably in their seats. "Trolls are not solitary beings. They live in family units. Parents. Children. The adults know better and are not easily tricked, but the children…" Caroline's eyes grow wide as she looks down at the stone in her hand, then back up at Jonas' grandmother.

The silverware begins to tremble, almost imperceptibly at first. As the tremors become more pronounced, it begins to feel as though the whole house exists inside of a shaken snow globe.

"Gram, what's happening?" Jonas asks, the panic rising in his voice. With an ear-splitting bang, the front door is blown off its hinges, shards of wood slicing through the air like razorblades. The family scatters to the far corners of the room, all eyes on the doorway as they gape at the unthinkable.

A troll—impossibly even larger than the one Jonas encountered—ducks inside with an exhale. The stench of dead fish and human sweat fills the room; an olfactory assault so overwhelming that Jonas struggles to keep the bile from rising to his throat. His aunt begins screaming so deafeningly, his eyes dart to her with a silent plea to keep quiet, but it's too late. The troll lifts one giant palm and brings it down on her head, as casually as a human swatting a fly. Jonas watches as her skull seems to liquefy with a sickening squelch.

Searching the room for anything he can use as a weapon, Jonas is stopped in his tracks when a second troll ducks through the open doorway. This one baring its rotten teeth, hairs stuck between them as if it has been eating along the way. It licks its lips before walking forward, and with a flick of its wrist throws the entire dining table into the air. It crashes down, landing on a few family members who had been trying to run away. The other troll trudges on top of the overturned table, and the sound of wood splintering and bones crunching is nauseating. Jonas vomits on himself, as Ingrid falls to her knees nearby.

"Give them the heart!" Ingrid bellows above the chaos. Caroline realizes she is still holding the emerald stone, and with a glance toward Jonas she tosses it as far away as she is able. One troll turns, its eyes locking on Ingrid, and it moves with surprising speed across the room. Ingrid's head is instantly crushed by the force of its hands, one bulging eyeball managing to roll across the floor to Jonas' feet.

Caroline appears next to Jonas and grabs his trembling hand, no words necessary for what's to come. Jonas lets out a thunderous scream as he grabs onto her. Both trolls now turn in their direction and start lumbering toward them—taking their time. Caroline shakes uncontrollably, as one of the trolls lowers its face to hers, its black eyes searching her expression. "Please," Caroline implores, as her legs give way beneath her. Jonas falls to the ground at her side.

"I'm sorry," he whispers. "Forgive me. Please forgive me. Forgive me…" It's unclear whether he is beseeching Caroline, or the trolls. With two massive fingers, one of the trolls reaches deep into Caroline's chest. Her mouth drops open in shock, hands feebly reaching up to stop something that there's no way to stop. Jonas cries out in horror as the troll pulls Caroline's still-beating heart from her chest, popping it in its mouth like hard candy. Caroline's limp body crumples to the floor, and Jonas throws himself on top of her, overcome by anguish. Beneath the shadow of a blistered foot, Jonas embraces his love for just a moment before the troll's leg slams down, rendering the pair an indiscernible puddle of blood and viscera.

The trolls scan the room until one of them sees what they're looking for—a glint of green that has rolled underneath a fallen chandelier. Clutching their child's heart between their hands in a private moment of sorrow, the trolls throw their heads back in the air, and they wail.

Her Best Life

Frances Howard-Snyder

Hedonist | A Tail

The classroom overlooked an emerald lawn with giant maples. Afternoon light falling from high windows illuminated the chalk particles that swirled above the slouching students. Professor Eloise Carter stood at the front of the room and clicked on her PowerPoint. "Hedonism," she said, in her deep, resonant professor's voice, "Is a view held by Jeremy Bentham and John Stuart Mill, the view that the only thing of intrinsic value is pleasure and the absence of pain."

"That sounds really selfish," one of the students piped up.

Eloise smiled. "Not necessarily. You *could* combine hedonism with egoism and be committed solely to your own pleasure. In which case, you would be selfish. But Bentham and Mill were utilitarians, who believed that pleasure was the only good, but that our obligation was to maximize it across the population. They believed in promoting the greatest good for the greatest number. If someone followed that theory consistently, they would be exactly the opposite of selfish."

The students scratched in their notebooks but did not look impressed.

"We will return to utilitarianism next week. Today I want to focus on hedonism– the theory that pleasure is the only truly valuable thing. Let's consider a thought experiment." She described Robert Nozick's Experience machine, mentioned its antecedents in Descartes's Evil Demon hypothesis, and told them it was like *The Matrix*, a reference she realized was out of date; many of them hadn't been born when The Matrix came out.

"The point of the machine is to maximize the subject's pleasurable experiences. Nozick's point is that life on the machine is second-rate. Even though you get more pleasure than you would off the machine, your life is deficient because it's an illusion, none of your deepest desires are satisfied, you're not making an impact on the world, you're not connected to any other people. No-one loves you. Nozick concludes that hedonism is false. Other things, like truth and love, are intrinsically valuable."

She glanced around the room, at the two dozen mostly young men and women in her 112, Ethics and the Good Life class. "So, which of you would choose to go on the machine? Let's suppose that once you've made the choice, you would forget that you'd made it and just experience a virtual reality for decades that gave you the sense that things were maximally perfect. You'd have the experience of being married to your dream person, following a dream career, winning all sorts of awards, living in a big house, travelling, whatever floats your boat, but it would all be an illusion."

The students glanced around, unsure whether they had understood, or uncomfortable about exposing their values. Then one hand went up, the handsome, older student in the back in a jacket and tie.

"So, you're a hedonist, Jason. You would choose to go on the machine?" she asked. "Can you explain why?"

"You never realize you're in the simulation, right?"

She nodded.

He reached into his jacket pocket, pulled something out, and tossed it. The coin caught the light in a distracting way. He did it again. And again. "So, what you don't know doesn't hurt you. you'd be having all that good stuff – great partner, great job and so on. With none of the shit in your current life? You bet I'd sign up." He kept tossing. "It comes down to a choice between pleasure." He tossed. As the coin hung in the air, he added, "And truth. Heads or tails."

"Stop that, please," she said. "I suppose you could put it like that."

"Who knows whether we're not in a simulation right now," a young woman with a ponytail said without raising her hand.

Eloise turned to her. "Sure. But wouldn't you *prefer* it if you weren't? Doesn't that tell you something about your own values?" Out of the corner of her eye, she noticed Jason toss his coin again.

"Yeah, but…" another young woman in a football jersey said. "…If you think you're married to a hot guy with great kids and a fantastic job, then that's your reality. So, what's the difference?"

Oh, no. Eloise had thought she'd cured them of the absurd "true for you, but not for me," relativism.

More and more hands went up. Jason was winning them over.

Eloise tried a few more argumentative moves; then she glanced at the clock. Two minutes to the end of the lesson. She didn't really need to convince them that Nozick was right – just to show them the implications of hedonism. She gave them a homework assignment to carefully lay out Nozick's argument and to indicate whether they agreed with him and say why or why not.

She thought about the class as she walked across campus towards her car. Sure, she imagined saying to Jason, a person with a very horrible life, who was being tortured or starving, could rationally choose the simulation, but if you start with a pretty good life…"

But then she wondered. Maybe Jason had a horrible life – maybe he was homeless or gripped by devastating depression. Maybe in his case, hedonism would make sense.

Her own life was pretty good, she reflected with satisfaction. She had a kind, nice-looking husband, a steady, well-paid job as a professor and researcher, a beautiful Siamese cat, and two perfect children, Stephen, who was in graduate school in Copenhagen, studying physics, and Agnes, who was studying linguistics at Oberlin. Both texted her every day. They loved her, she knew, and she loved them more than life itself. Her parents were well and financially secure, her friends, fun and interesting, and she herself was healthy and in good shape. She'd had some small disappointments, of course. She could certainly imagine increasing the pleasure in her life but she wouldn't exchange our own rich and fulfilling existence for maximized pleasure on the experience machine.

Her husband was on a trip to Chicago, so she had the house to herself. After grading and watching a couple of episodes of *Black Mirror*, she fell asleep with her cat on the pillow beside her, its tail twitching restlessly.

She woke in the deepest part of the night. Her room looked different; she heard odd sounds, the whirring of machines, the sounds of people moving. Needing to pee, she climbed out of bed but fell on a linoleum floor. Her bed was higher than she remembered it and her body was numb and stiff. What was going on?

She found the door and walked in a long, dimly lit corridor. Where was she? Not at home obviously. She must have had some sort of medical event and been rushed to hospital. She needed to find out what was going on. What was wrong with her? Where was she? Had her family been notified? Where were they?

She heard whispering and discerned snatches of conversation: "Breakdown... power outage."

"We need to keep them asleep."

"Why? If they wake, we can just erase their memories." One of the voices sounded familiar.

She rounded a corner and saw through an open door a group of people in white coats – The one in the middle reminded her of her student, Jason. Good grief! It was Jason. He must be a nurse or orderly.

He smiled at her. "Professor!" he said, and then turned to the group and laughed heartily.

"Jason. Can you tell me what's happening? I have no idea what's going on."

He tossed his coin.

She remembered him doing this in class. Heads: pleasure; tails: truth. She spoke louder. "Jason. I'm your professor. What is going on? I insist you tell me the truth." Her voice sounded thin and shrill, nothing like her normal voice.

He laughed again. "You're not really my professor. Or anyone's professor."

She blinked at him. Was he joking, teasing, toying with her? That was not nice. She'd make him pay when it came to final grades.

He walked over and took her arm, an arm that looked thinner and paler than she remembered.

"Let's get you back to bed, shall we?" He led her past rooms filled with rows of beds, each containing a patient with electrodes attached to a shaved skull. Beside them machines whirred and beeped. The patients' eyes were closed but their mouths were twisted in beatific smiles, roars of delight, or moments of ecstasy.

"Wait," she said, touching her own head, which was also shaven. "What is happening to me? Where is my husband? Where are my children?"

He laughed. "That's a very long story. One I don't have time for right now. I have a crisis of my own to deal with." He pushed her through a door and down onto an empty bed, and then deftly inserted a needle in her arm.

Her children—she thought as she drifted into sleep, her beautiful Agnes and Stephen—were they also lying prostrate on beds somewhere, not living their best lives but forever asleep, passively dreaming, unaware of her existence. Or – even worse – could it be that Agnes and Stephen did not exist—at least, not as flesh and blood people but merely as figments of her imagination with no consciousness, no life, no pleasure of their own, no love? She felt a pulse of agony before her mind went dark.

"I had a dream last night," she told her class, trying to infuse an upbeat note into her voice. "I dreamt I was in a simulation and I woke up."

"I thought you said people in the simulation never woke up," one of her students objected.

"If you did wake up and realized that your whole life was fake, that you weren't married to Taylor Swift and the president of the United States, then it wouldn't be a counterexample to hedonism, would it? Because you'd be miserable," another pointed out.
"Excellent point," Eloise said. "But ask yourself—*why* would you be miserable? If you knew that your entire life had been full of pleasure and if you thought that pleasure was the only thing that mattered. As a hedonist, you should recognize that your life had been the best possible life. So, why feel sad?"

The student frowned and tipped his head.

Jason tossed his coin again. It caught the light and for a fraction of a second, Eloise's vision froze, like a zoom screen, students' face stuck in absurd expressions. The coin landed. Everything was back to normal. He did it again. Again, the world lurched: she saw black with a buffering circle. Was she losing her mind?

Then everything was normal again. Was her vision failing? Was she having a stroke? Or was it something far, far more terrifying.

Jason tossed again.

"Heads," she called, as if her life depended on it. "I choose heads."

Jason slapped the coin on the back of his hand. "You can bet, but you cannot choose."

The idea that he was making this happen was absurd. But she wanted to make him stop. She wanted to take the coin away from him, give him an F, expel him from her class.

She pinched herself until she felt a bruise. Did that mean she wasn't dreaming? No. Dreams could have pinches in them, especially the sort of dreams imagined by Descartes and Nozick. Dreams could have dreams in them.

Then she was lying horizontal and Jason was beside her. The beds were high so he wouldn't have to bend. He took her wrist and she felt the sweet sting of the needle.

How Fast They Run

Charlie Rogers

Hiker | Hole

10:16 a.m.

I keep my eye on the side view mirror and watch the shrinking city vanish as we curve around the mountain. The expansive fields of swaying brown, dried under an unforgiving sun, disappear as well, replaced by jagged gray stone.

"You awake, Jimmy? You're being awful quiet." Derrick turns up the music as though admitting he doesn't care to hear my response.

I can barely look at him after what I discovered this morning.

Derrick's expensive electric car rumbles noisily over gravel as we enter a small, empty lot. He shifts into park and grins at me. I force myself to reciprocate but I'm stuck thinking about the photo roll on his phone. So many dick pictures. Orifices that definitely weren't mine, or his. And videos whose graphic thumbnails assured me I wasn't paranoid.

I'll confront him tonight, or, I don't know, maybe tomorrow. But not now.

10:32 a.m.

Derrick pauses to photograph a rock formation that he claims resembles me, and I press on ahead, still flipping through his illicit images in my mind.

It was probably a mistake to join him on this hike, but I was so stunned by what I'd uncovered that I wasn't thinking clearly, and he was so excited for it. It's all he's talked about all week. The magical hiking spot he found on the internet. The swimming hole. I was enthusiastic, too, until this morning.

He sprints to catch up with me and grabs my side, nuzzling into my neck. His beard tickles and I can't help but laugh.

"There's my Jimmy!" He lifts his face to mine.

I smile, wondering if he can see how forced the expression is, or if I'm fooling him as he's fooled me for months. "I'm right here."

Derrick sighs, satisfied. He's so handsome, with his dark, chiseled features, though when he smiles, his teeth are too big and one of his canines sits slightly akimbo.

He grabs for my hand. "C'mon. We're almost to the hole."

I don't think I can handle this charade much longer.

10:47 a.m.

I have to admit the swimming hole is a magnificent find, a grotto carved out of sedimentary stone where a small, restless pool bubbles beneath a rumbling waterfall. It's much cooler here than it was on the path.

"I don't know if I want to actually swim." I set my backpack beside a tree, grateful to be free of its weight.

Derrick sets his beneath a different tree, a few feet away. He grins at me, flashing the imperfect tooth that somehow makes the rest of his face even more attractive, and whips off his tanktop. He laughs as he tosses it at me. "C'mon!"

A wave of insecurity hits me. Maybe I'm *no fun?* Maybe that's why Derrick's been cheating?

Fine.

When I remove my t-shirt the mist rising off the pool raises goosebumps on my arms. I feel hideous next to beautiful Derrick, exposed and vulnerable. Meanwhile he kicks his sneakers in my direction then lets his shorts drop to his ankles.

"What if someone else comes by?" I glance in both directions on the path.

"Do you see anyone else?" Derrick shakes his head. "When did you get so shy?"

I pull a deep inhale. "I'm not, I just…"

When he approaches me for a kiss, I can't let on how little I want to taste his minty tongue, so I don't resist.

"You've got nothing to be ashamed of." He runs his callused palms along my arms. "But fine. We'll keep our undies on."

I open my mouth to speak. I need to confront him. But all I say is, "Okay."

He nods, then strolls to the water's edge. I watch him go, and for a moment, I let myself forget my pain, my feelings of betrayal, and let my affection for him bubble back. "Derrick, c'mere."

He turns with a sly smile.

I'm not sure if I want to kiss him or slap his almost-perfect face.

I don't need to decide.

The ground roils beneath us, like I'm standing on a floating dock. I instinctively shoot my arms out for balance and I peer down at my shoes, as if they'll bring me extra stability.

"Earthquake? Holy fuck." Derrick's voice quavers.

Another rumble follows. Derrick calls out, an unintelligible yelp.

When I lift my head, he's gone.

10:53 a.m.

The hole that swallowed Derrick is about two feet wide, a rough oval.

"Derrick!" I lean over the edge, nervous to stand too close as it might further crumble.

"I'm fine!" He doesn't sound far away but the hole is pitch black. "Fucked up my ankle maybe, but I'm fine."

"Can you climb out?" I shine the flashlight on my phone into the darkness but still don't see him.

I hear Derrick grunt, then swear. "I don't think so. Too tough to get a foothold. There's rope in the car."

"I'll be right back!" Though we both know how far away the car is.

11:41 a.m.

I don't notice the other holes in the ground on my jog downhill to the lot. Only as I'm returning with the heavy coil of rope hanging off my shoulder, running uphill, that I begin spotting them dotting the sides of the path. They're all about the same size, and at some point I start counting. I notch a half dozen before I'm back at the swimming spot.

"I'm back!" I call into the hole and hustle over to the closest, strongest-looking tree. My dad had taught me about all kinds of knots when I was a kid, and the memory returns in fits before I settle on a basic bowline, cinched around the old sycamore.

I toss the other end into the hole.

It's still quiet down there and I panic that there wasn't enough play to reach the ground. "Derrick? Do you see the rope?"

He doesn't answer.

I shine the light again, somehow expecting to see anything other than black.

"Derrick?"

Maybe he fell asleep down there?

I try calling his name a few more times, then yank the extended rope back up. Without allowing time to talk myself out of this, I wrap the line around my waist, knot it tight, gather up the slack, and lower myself into the hole. I grip the taut rope with one hand, gather a fistful of the slack, then let the taut side free, over and over, dropping a few feet at a time.

As I descend, a foul odor rises to greet me, a dry mustiness mingled with a sharp scent, maybe rot. I catch myself holding my breath to avoid it.

Whenever I'm able to find a decent foothold in the jagged rock, I pause to shine the flashlight into the pit. The darkness seems stubborn, as though it doesn't want me to see what's down there.

I *hear* something, though. At first I think it's Derrick babbling to himself, then it sounds like running water. As I grow closer the noise resembles someone slurping cereal, a slightly nauseating sound.

I shine the light again and I finally see Derrick, leaning against the opposite wall. His eyes are open, wide, dark orbs that shine my light back at me, but he doesn't respond to my sudden appearance as I dangle ten feet above him.

Then I see them.

Pale, scaly claws grip his biceps while others encircle his waist.

What are they?

I shine the flashlight across Derrick's body and notice movement in his chest. Is his heart beating that hard? Or—?

The skin splits open in a rain of blood.

A fanged snout bursts through, chomping at the air.

Oh fuck.

My phone slips from my hand as I scramble, grasping for a higher handhold to hoist myself out of the pit. I hear Derrick's body *thump* as whatever was holding him lets him collapse to the ground, followed by a low hiss.

I grip the rope and yank myself up. The opening is closer than I realized, inspiring me to push myself, faster, further, up towards my escape. I don't look down. I can't.

11:49 a.m.

As I hoist myself back to solid ground, the creature swipes at my foot. I didn't even realize it was scaling the wall, chasing me, but I'm able to wrap my fingers around an exposed root and yank myself to temporary safety.

I abandon everything we brought and start to sprint. I doubt I'll be able to maintain this pace for the entire trip back to the car, but maybe if I get enough distance the creature will abandon its pursuit.

Back on the trail, I remember all the other holes I spotted on my way to try rescuing Derrick. There's no time to think about it. I see a frantic young woman running up the trail in my direction.

"Hello? Please help!"

Before I'm able to even attempt a response, a second creature tackles her from behind, chomping on her neck. It looks up at me greedily, a bloody fragment of the woman's spine dangling from its maw, its eyes blacker than obsidian, its scales the color of curdled milk.

I have no choice but to charge past it.

As I cut a wide circle around it, the creature returns its attention to its prey, gnawing a sizable hole in the back of her skull. I hear her bones crunch in its jaw.

Only then do I chance a glance back.

Four creatures follow me, scrabbling along the trail. One stops to chomp the woman's leg while the others, including the blood-covered beast that killed Derrick, continue their pursuit of me. They resemble albino alligators but their bodies are narrower, their legs longer; if not for their protruding reptile snouts they could be mistaken for primates, galloping on all fours.

It's not far now. I grip Derrick's car keys in my fist. I can make it.

The torso of a young man marks the end of the trail. All his limbs are missing, spurs of bone jutting from his joints like mistakes. I suspect he was with the woman I encountered but it doesn't matter. His car is parked next to Derrick's.

My legs feel like lit matches and I can barely breathe, my heart thundering like an angry storm, but I'm so close. I jam the button to unlock Derrick's car, the incongruous double-beep a muffled shout from a previous life, and circle around the other vehicle.

The creature that ate the man I just passed pops out from underneath the other car, rearing onto its hind legs like a vicious, blood-splattered kangaroo. It swipes for me with its stiletto claws.

I dodge its initial attack and punch its long throat, Derrick's key poking between my knuckles. The key doesn't puncture its leathery skin, but knocks it off balance enough that I'm able to throw open the car door as a barrier between us, and hurl myself inside.

Safety.

Derrick's music—a decades-old pop song—blasts the moment I turn over the engine and I start to laugh, a spurt of a giggle erupting into uncontrollable hysterics. As more of the monsters, at least ten, emerge from the trail or clamber from unseen holes, all I can do is cackle at the absurdity of this, pounding the dashboard and seat beside me.

Then I gather a calming breath and flip off the music. I never liked this song anyway.

The creatures watch me.

I could toss the car in reverse and book it towards home. I could pray that the city isn't also overrun with these subterranean reptile-men and try to return to a semblance of a normal life without Derrick.

I think of him, lying dead in that pit. Rage bubbles underneath my skin.

My other option is to go forward, towards the waiting creatures, and see how fast they can really run.

The choice is clear.

Author Biographies

Bryan Arneson
Necromancy, And Other Fun Games You Can Play
Bryan Arneson writes genre fiction from the Gulf Coast with his partner and two cats, Navi and Merlin. By day, he is a freelance editor and ghostwriter, and he can be reached at @ArnesonAuthor on X (Twitter) or by trading a syllable of your name to the denizens of the new moon.

Kat Veldt
Form Of
Kat Veldt was detasseled from the cornfields of Iowa and scattered across the contiguous States before putting down roots in the Twin Cities with their daughters (feline). They write weird fiction, study library and information science, and drink a lot of tea. You can find them at http://katpla.net and on instagram @veldtkat.

MM Schreier
The Vast Enormity of the Sea
MM Schreier is a classically trained vocalist who took up writing as therapy for a mid-life crisis. Whether contemporary or speculative fiction, favorite stories are rich in sensory details and weird twists. A firm believer that people are not always exclusively right- or left-brained, in addition to creative pursuits, Schreier is on the Leadership Team for a robotics company and tutors maths and science to at-risk youth. Follow in the web: mmschreier.com

Lisa Short
Jammed
Lisa Short is a Texas-born, Kansas-bred writer of fantasy, science fiction and horror. She has an honorable discharge from the United States Army, a degree in chemical engineering, and twenty years' experience as a professional engineer. Lisa currently lives in Maryland with her husband, youngest child, father-in-law, two cats and a puppy. She can be found online and on Bluesky at

lisashortauthor.com and on Twitter and Instagram
@Lisa_K_Short.

Michael Boulerice
Deli Meat
Michael Boulerice hails from the wilds of New Hampshire. When
he's not pouring his greatest fears into a keyboard, Michael is either
snowboarding in the White Mountains, or spoiling his pets rotten.

Rory Clark
Hej, Eina!
Rory Clark is a Logistics Shift Manager from London and a
fledgling writer. A full time enjoyer of spirits, and a part time hive-
mind. You can find him trying to enter your dreams through your
ear.

Josephine Queen
Those Useless Things
Josephine grew up in England, but has spent most of her adult life
in New England. As a child she was disappointed by the lack of
magical worlds behind wardrobe doors, so decided to create her
own with words when she was nine-years-old. A "few" decades
and many imagined worlds later, some of those words have been
published in various online and print anthologies, including Spread:
Tales of Deadly Flora edited by R. A. Clarke and Spirits and
Ghouls Short Stories by Flame Tree Publishers. Josephine is
currently working on a rewrite of a middle-grade novel she hopes
her nine-year-old self would be proud of. She still lives in New
England, a place that provides the perfect inspiration for the
spooky stories she tends to write.

Pete Neilsen
Gifts From Above
Pete Neilsen has had six decades of the real world to appreciate
immersing himself in weird forests with telepathic panthers as
family members. I mean, much cooler, right? With thanks to
TL;DR Press, this is his first published story. *(it's our pleasure, Pete!)*

Mason Yeater
The Love Theatre
Mason Yeater writes speculative fiction near the Great Lakes. Previously his work has been published in *TL;DR Press'* Curios anthology, and is forthcoming in Diabolical Plots. He can be found sometimes @snow_leeks on Twitter.

Jonathan M. Wolf
The Vault
Jonathan M. Wolf lives in the suburbs of Chicago, IL with his wife and three kids. He works as a video editor, and loves telling stories (although typically science fiction). He plays a lot of board games, builds LEGO, and designs things with his 3D printer, finding inspiration in the stories that are created around the gaming (and hobby-ing) table.

Aggie Novak
The Translation of Nina
Aggie lives with her wife by the beach in Australia, where she spends most of her time hiding from the sun and heat. She writes around studying for her pharmacy degree and entertaining her three dogs. She loves all kinds of speculative fiction and often draws inspiration from Slavic folklore and mythology. When not writing she can be found drinking tea and reading everything in sight.

Sean Fallon
The Dog in the Glass Jar
Sean currently writes for Film Inquiry, a movie and TV criticism website, and Hard Drive/Hard Times, satirical pop culture news sites. His fiction writing has been featured in numerous anthologies, websites and publications including the Big Issue and Readers Digest. He lives in Melbourne, Australia with his wife and son.

Nicole Lovell
Into the Gray
Nicole Lovell is from the suburbs of Chicago, where her exposure to diversity and culture heavily influenced her interest in the world at large. She credits her grandfather for sparking her interest in reading and story telling. She fondly recalls dictating a story to him at age three, which he bound into her very first book with scrap paper and staples. When she isn't reading or writing, she's absorbed in world issues, playing board games, learning piano, or talking to trees. Nicole and her wife reside happily in Northern Illinois with their pets and family. Keep an eye out for her queer romance novels in 2025.

Clive Wallis
For When You Want Something Special
Clive Wallis is a graduate of the University of York. He worked for years in the technology sector before retraining as a teacher in 2011. He is currently a secondary school librarian in a town on the Dorset coast. He is married with two teenage sons and the world's smallest miniature Schnauzer.

Ana Nelson
The Friends We Keep
Ana Nelson lives in Minnesota with her cat, Giggles. When she's not sleeping, she can be found writing, playing cello, or playing Pokémon (even though she's 26).

Victoria Higgins
What Did They Do to You?
Victoria is a writer in South London. You can find her on Twitter @liqorise.

Nicoletta Giuseffi
Out of Mind
Nicoletta Giuseffi is a pansexual English language professor and princess under glass. Her work appears in publications like Moonflowers & Nightshade and Mother: Tales of Love and Terror, which was nominated for a 2022 Bram Stoker Award. She has also

received the Elegant Literature Prize. Her passions include photography, retro hardware, and the late 18th century.

David Cotton
In the Dark, Nothing Flowers
David Cotton lives in Cardiff, Wales, with his wife, two children, an elderly guinea-pig and many soft toy animals. He was the first lead builder for the online text game Lusternia: Age of Ascension, and particularly enjoyed writing for the d`ark forest Glomdoring. When he's not playing games, reading manga or watching surgical operations, David occasionally writes stories.

Madeleine Pelletier
Unchained
Madeleine Pelletier lives in a farmhouse near Montreal with three cats, six goats and one grumpy old man. Her work has been featured in The Arcanist, Sundial, and Janus Literary, among others. Follow her on X @mad_pelletier and Bluesky @madpelletier.bsky.social.

Thomas Farr
Ozymandias
Thomas Farr is a British writer and poet whose work appears or is forthcoming in Tales to Terrify, Ram Eye Press, River Heron Review, Aôthen Magazine, Wales Haiku Journal, Kyoto Journal and elsewhere. If he isn't writing, he's probably running or talking to his plants. He tweets [X's] @tfarrpoetry.

Linda M. Bayley
Money, Beauty, and Brains
Linda M. Bayley is a writer and textile artist living on the Canadian Shield. Her work has appeared in Geist, The Windsor Review, Open Minds Quarterly, and voidspace zine. You can find her on Twitter/X @lmbayley.

Ash Egan
The Last Picture
Ash Egan began writing horror stories in 2022. He lives in Bury, in the north of England.

Heather Scott
The Final Course
Heather Scott is an art teacher who recently rediscovered her love of writing, and now teaches creative writing to middle and high school students. Horror and thriller are her favorite genres to write, but she's found that she also enjoys writing romantic comedies every now and then. A lifelong learner and lover of books, her next goal is to complete and publish her first novel. When not teaching, writing, or teaching writing, she loves to spend time with her husband and their 5-year-old daughter.

Frances Howard-Snyder
Her Best Life
Frances Howard-Snyder is a philosophy professor at Western Washington University. She has an MFA from the Rainier Writing Workshop, and has published short stories in The Magnolia Review, Silver Pen, Marrow Magazine, Halfway down the Stairs, and numerous other places. She is working on a novel. When not reading or writing, she can be found walking in the forest or hanging out with friends and family.

Charlie Rogers
How Fast They Run
Charlie Rogers is a random assemblage of atoms and other parts that mostly exists in New York City, writing the same story over and over, ignoring birds and their portents. There's a website, too: http://www.charlierogerswrites.com

Judges

Callum Rowland

Callum is a fiction writer, and co-founder of *TL;DR Press*. He writes across all genres; though science fiction, fantasy, and horror are closest to his heart. His short stories have featured in various magazines, anthologies, and zines, including Daily Science Fiction, Fictive Dream, Aphelion Webzine, and Bandit Fiction. He is Director of Charity for *TL;DR Press*, and has also worked as either a curator or editor on a number of TL;DR releases, most recently as a curator on Growth.

Joe Butler

Joe lives and works in London, but dreams of living and working elsewhere. He is the author of three novels, *Of All Possibilities, Strange Days in the House of August*, and his forthcoming book, *A Home for Grief* published by Diachroneity Books. His short fiction has been featured in Hexagon, Bandit Fiction, Ghost Orchid, Second Chance Lit, and the Found anthology edited by Gabino Iglesias and Andrew Cull. He can be found on twitter at @writelikeashark and on his website www.writelikeashark.com. He is one of the co-founders of *TL;DR Press*, and has been involved in all of the collections the press has published as either a curator or an editor as well as the marketing manager and cover artist for eight of the ten currently released collections. He has also been one of the judges for all of the previous 1KWHC competitions.

Penfold

Penfold is a writer, software security engineer, and semicolon enthusiast. He is a founding member of TL;DR Press and has served as curator and editor on various anthologies, as well as judge in the previous 1KWHC contests. He lives near Indianapolis with his wife, two kids, and a number of cats as ever-changing as the sea. He is currently writing a collection of stories about the slow-burning insanity of raising an international family in the lawless, feral suburbs of the midwest. His stories have appeared in previous TL;DR Press anthologies, and he can be found and interrogated at www.justpenfold.com or on Twitter at @justpenfold.

Jenna Harvie

Jenna Harvie is a writer, painter, and photographer from Atlantic Canada. She spends her days writing and editing technical documents for a cybersecurity company and her evenings working on her own fiction, editing, and reading anything she can get her hands on. Jenna is currently editing her first horror novel, writing a few more, and she always has a short story or two on the go. Jenna has been editing and judging for TL;DR Press since 2019, and she is also on the Board of Directors. And when that's not enough, she paints landscapes and abstractions and photographs the beautiful landscape around Nova Scotia. Visit Jenna's art gallery online at https://jennaharvie.com/ or find her on Instagram with the handle @jennaharvie.

Mia V. Moss

Mia V. Moss is a speculative fiction author from the Pacific Northwest, now living in the SF Bay area. She is the author of the sci-fi noir novella Mai Tais for the Lost. Her short stories have been published in Cat Ladies of the Apocalypse, StarShipSofa, Galactic Stew, and elsewhere. Mia is currently working on an epic fantasy series. When she's not writing, she DMs tabletop campaigns, wildscapes her yard, and admires her ever-growing TBR pile. She can be reached at www.magicrobotcarnival.com or on Instagram @atomicjackalope.

Hannah Hulbert

Hannah Hulbert is a full-time mum and part-time writer from the south coast of England. She enjoys looking for mushrooms, doing crafts, and drinking tea, especially when she is supposed to be writing. You can find her stories in Metaphorosis, Hexagon, and the anthology Cat Ladies of the Apocalypse, among others. Her story 'Ruler of Waves, God of Trees' from Growth (*TL;DR Press*, 2021), received a Pushcart nomination. You can find her via her website, https://hannahhulbert.wordpress.com/

About TL;DR Press

TL;DR Press is a 501(c)3 charity founded in 2017 to uplift writers around the world for a good cause. United under the belief that writing can impact the world, we have made it our mission to help both writers and charities with the power of the written word. Our goals are:

- Create a writing community that fosters an atmosphere of supportiveness and collaboration. By working together, we help authors hone their craft and find a welcoming place to share their work.

- Help good causes gain more attention and support through the promotion of our anthologies. All proceeds to each of our anthologies goes to charity, and we are proud of the partnerships that we have forged to help create a better world—one word at a time.

Want to join in on the fun or learn more about our mission? Please visit us at tldrpress.org.

Printed in Great Britain
by Amazon